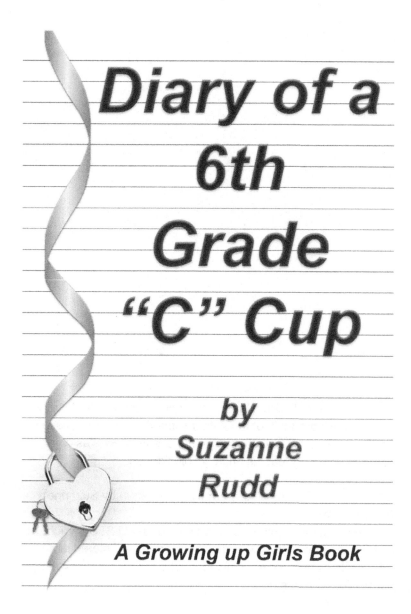

Diary of a 6th Grade "C" Cup

by
Suzanne
Rudd

A Growing up Girls Book

Why This Story?

I wrote this book to tell the tale of the tormented silent minority. No one ever exposes the perils of girls who develop early. Society looks at bombshells with big chests as the "lucky" few. But having "big boobs" isn't all it's cracked up to be. They don't know the cost in ridicule, embarrassment, and humiliation that can erode the very delicate beginnings of self-esteem. Girls can be mean and boys can be really stupid. This is bullying, plain and simple. Those who prop themselves up on the backs of those who are different to make themselves feel better choose the dark side of mental abuse. If bullies win, their prey is a victim. Overcoming that situation makes you stronger and gain the self-confidence skills needed to fight peer pressure and stay on the right track to succeed in the challenges of life.

I went through many similar circumstances as one of the few who developed early in life. Many of the stories are based on my own personal experiences and those of others I knew who experienced similar humiliations.

Growing up isn't easy. It's full of difficulty, obstacles, and peril around every corner. But it's also new and exciting. Everything is a first. It's definitely a roller coaster ride. But the test is not to get off the ride. Ride again and again. Don't get off just because you think you will throw up; drink some water and go again until you enjoy it. And don't let anyone make you stop enjoying the ride.

Why Bully?

"If you read up on the causes of bullying there many articles which discuss the lack of ability to recognize distress in others and the problems with anger and behavioral disruption kids experience that leads to bullying behaviors. What I believe happens on a more frequent basis and what I see happening in the lives of my clients, my child, and what I experienced as a kid are the microaggressions that build up and cause harm. It is the whispered comments, the looks given, and the nicknames given that the building hurt and harm is found. The statement often put out there is kids are mean. The question less asked is where does that meanness come from? Sometimes it comes from the environment; the child sees it or hears it and they mimic it, not understanding the full gravity of their doing. Other times it is a fear or weakness that drives it. What I can say definitively affects it is how this is addressed by parents, primary schools, and everyone as you get older. If kids are taught to be kind, to be aware of differences in a way that evokes compassion, not judgement or weirdness, these things would happen less. The struggle is when parents do not know how to do this, how would we teach the children? Start with the recognition that everyone is different. Lead with the introduction that this is beautiful, not wrong."

Sarah Decker,
Licensed Marriage and Family Therapist

With Love and Appreciation...

This book is dedicated to everyone in my family and friends who helped me knock down the obstacles, jump over the hurdles, leap ahead, and pick me up each time I got knocked down.

Thanks to my "Pens" friends and colleagues for your encouragement and direction, especially my friend and mentor, author J.E. Marksteiner, who put me on the right track and helped me realize this story after 40 years in the making. And to my editor Judy Loose (J.C. Ferguson), who is my safety net.

Special thanks to author Judy Blume who showed me the way through her books when I was growing up and motivated me to tell the ever-important stories of the underdogs.

Dedication

A shout out to the late great RBG, Supreme Court Justice Ruth Bader Ginsburg, who passed away just before the printing of this book. She was a shining light who focused a spotlight that never flickered on the rights of the oppressed, different, ignored, and disenfranchised. She was an unwavering icon who tirelessly championed equality for all. She ingeniously paved the way for all little girls, young women of all races, religions, and preference to know that they can achieve anything. She inspired everyone to look up and see; there is only a ceiling if you see one.

"Reading is the key that opens doors to shape many good things in life. Reading shaped my dreams and more. Reading helped me make my dreams come true."
Ruth Bader Ginsburg 1933-2020

Suzanne Rudd

4th Grade

No Bra: Free and Easy

Dear RBG:

My grandma says everyone has their crosses to bear in life. Some people think their hair is too flat or too curly, or that they are too fat or too skinny or too tall or too short. After all, almost no one I know completely loves the way they look, especially when they're growing up. It's always too much or little of this or that.

My problem is—my boobs are too big. I know, I know, most girls envy that problem, some grown women too. I see my friends clasp their hands together in front of their chest, pressing together while chanting, "I must, I must, I must increase my bust." Or they wear padded bras or stuff them with tissue or rolled-up socks—weird, but kinda funny. To my knowledge, none of these works. But if it did, they would understand that even crosses that seem sent from heaven all have a little devil in them.

My name is Katie R. Sorry, Katie Reed. I'm used to writing Katie R. In my school, it's typical for kids with common names to have more than one Bobby, John, or Karen in the same class, so to avoid confusion, the teacher refers to us with our name and the first initial of our last name. I don't mind it too much, but it makes you hate having a common name. Every year, there's more than one Katie in my class, so I'm used to putting the last name initial on everyone's first name. A few times, I thought it would be fun to meld the two together and be called "Katier."

For my eleventh birthday, everyone gave me books. I like to read. My uncle gave me a book of important words called the "Superior Persons Book of Superfluous Words" and a book about you, Supreme Court Justice Ruth Bader Ginsburg. My uncle says the first book is full of $10, $20, and $25 words that will get me through life. I guess the "price" is a joke about the complexity of the word. And he said the book about you would show me how to live. I like that idea. He's a lawyer, but he calls himself a "people's advocate." He knows I want to be a lawyer when I grow up, or maybe an actress or model; I still haven't decided. After reading your story, I'm definitely leaning toward lawyer or judge. You were as tough as nails and didn't take crap from anybody, no matter what. Sometimes I wish I was that way.

My mom gave me a diary. She had one when she was my age, and it helped her during this "difficult period"—that's what she called it. I know, right, an actual written diary. Who does that? Some older kids post every thought and feeling that comes into their head on social media, but I'm too young for that. Most of my friends aren't on social media yet. I like the idea of a journal to write my thoughts down and clear my head. But writing in a book and to "Dear Diary" all the time seems so old-fashioned. I mean, who is dear diary? My mom bought me this book, so I should use it. But instead of diary, I'll write to you, my new favorite hero, Ruth Bader Ginsburg. You were so tough that you even had a nickname, "The Notorious RBG." Very cool.

Dear RBG:

Fourth Grade is rough. I'm sure you remember. Everything's changing. You're not a little kid anymore, but you're not a teen or even a pre-teen. I don't know if they even have a name for this age. Just kid, I guess. Over the summer, I had a huge growth spurt. I'm now five-foot-three-inches tall. Compared to many adults, this is not tall. But in fourth grade, it's tall and awkward.

My grandma says I'm blossoming into a flower. I sure don't feel as beautiful or as graceful as a flower.

Are there ugly flowers? Most of the time, I feel like a lowly green seed in the dirt, like in those potted gifts everyone always made for Mother's Day in first grade. Just an ugly seed stuck in the mud.

Now my flower seems to have buds. In Health class, they call it "puberty" or becoming a woman. I started my "womanhood" last week. I got my period. And even worse, it came at school. I got up for recess, and there was blood on my chair. Normally, I would've thought I was dying, but my mom also bought me a book about getting your period a few months ago, so I knew what it was. Thank God for that Judy Blume book. I looked it up online too, but it was confusing and didn't explain it much. Sometimes books are better than the internet.

Why did have to get it at school? How embarrassing. I didn't want anyone to know, so I stayed seated and told my friends I would catch up with them. Then I told my teacher, and she took me to the bathroom and then to the school nurse to get a tampon. They had some emergency underpants for this and other "accidental" occasions. Nothing got on my dress, so it could have been a lot worse. The school nurse showed me how to use a tampon. Yikes, it was hard and hurt a little bit, but the school nurse said I'd get used to it. I think the whole thing is gross and uncomfortable, but I'm sure you know that. You are probably used to it by now. I hope I will get used to it soon. I really thought I was too young to get it, but my grandma told me that every woman in our family is an early bloomer. Great.

And this week, I got boobs. They just sprouted up overnight. My grandma says things always happen in groups of three. I guess this is my third in the blossoming game - height, period, and boobs, like win, place or show if growing up was a horse race. It's not a big deal. I mean, I didn't think anything of it at first.

But today it became a big deal. We took our class picture. Most of the entire class stood on risers, and a few kids sat cross-legged on the ground and held a slate commemorating the class name and year. Did they do those in the "olden days" when you were in school? I bet your class picture was in black and white. I think they did that back then.

I'm now the second tallest kid in the class, and the photographer put me and some of the other girls, who also grew taller this year, in the back row. My mom says boys don't have their growth spurts until after eighth grade. I guess she's right because the entire back row was girls. But I hope she's wrong. I don't want to be looking down at boys for four more years, and even worse, I don't want them looking up at me.

My friend Sandy stood next to me. Sandy is really tall too, even taller than me. Plus, her hair is huge, curly, and frizzy, so she looks even taller. Most of the boys are about a head's height below us in the back row. And yes, it's the perfect spot for them to stare directly into my "blossoming bosom," as my grandma puts it. Turns out I'm the first in my class to get "boobies." Lucky me. When I grew a foot up, I think they grew a foot out—or maybe just half a foot. It's weird. No one else in my class has them.

We have thirty-two kids in our class. My teacher says our school is overcrowded because of all the new houses going up in the neighborhood. So, we were squished really tight to get everyone in the picture. I heard some snickering and saw a couple of the boys in front of me, turning around one by one and then turning back and laughing to each other. This kid named Matt C. turned around, pointed at me, and said he could see THEM poking through my dress. He pulled his shirt out at the chest and laughed with the other boys and some of the girls. I looked down, and yes, my boobs were standing at attention, straight out under my dress and undershirt. It looked like the top of a tent. I wanted to jump off the riser and just run away. Boys are really stupid, and so are some girls. Sandy saw they were making fun of me, and she punched Matt C. in the arm and then looked at me and smiled. That did it; they all stopped laughing. The teacher didn't see anything. She was too busy getting the rest of the class to line up in the front rows. Sandy is always doing stuff like that to help me. She's a true best friend.

Dear RBG:

I wish these boobs never came in. I know all women get them, but at eleven years old? They make me feel more awkward and uncomfortable every day.

Especially in gym, when we have to change into our gym suits. They're these awful one-piece Kelly-green jumpers that snap up the top with elastic-bottom balloon-like shorts. I don't know why we wear this gym suit instead of shorts and a t-shirt, it looks like something from the old days. And of course, when you're "blossoming," the gym suit now barely fits in the chest, and there are gaps—big gaps. We all have to change in front of each other in the locker room. Anything new has a spotlight on it, and they'll definitely all look at my boobs, even just out of curiosity.

Sure enough, ALL the girls pointed and stared and snickered to each other, everyone except Sandy. She thinks it's no big deal. She says she has big hair, and I have boobs, so we all stick out somehow. She's great. When she sees the other girls staring at me, she stands in front of me to block their view. It helps, but sometimes I just wish I had one of those invisibility cloaks, so I could disappear in the locker room. If I could fit inside the locker, I would dress in there every day. I would love to tell them to get over it. After all, they'll have these someday too. But today I have them, and they don't.

Last week, I had an idea. I brought my gym suit home to be washed and then wore it underneath my clothes to school the next day. I wore a dress that day, so I didn't have to change. I could just take my dress off and then put it back on after gym. I thought the dress would hide the gym suit, but it didn't. It was bulky and very noticeable. You could tell I had something on underneath my dress. It looked weird, so they laughed all day instead of just at gym. I'm never doing that again.

Dear RBG:

School pictures came out today. I'm horrified. You could see my boobs right through my undershirt and dress. Not like an x-ray or anything, but they looked like two small cupcakes with cherries on top planted on my shirt. Of course, there was a round of snickering and giggling when everyone saw the picture. The whole class got that picture and will keep it forever. It will NEVER end.

When I showed the picture to my mom, she said it was time to get a bra. I barely know what that is, but I don't want one. I've seen ads for them, and they look like torture devices. At our family's annual Halloween parties, I've seen my mom's friends dress up in corseted pirate and witch costumes and even saw a lady once in a Playboy bunny costume. It didn't look comfortable at all. All night they tug on it and pull it up. Nope, not for me. I told my mom I don't think I need one. I mean I have boobs, but not like a Barbie doll. No one in my class has one, so I don't want one. But my boobs are starting to be noticable, and sometimes you can see them through my clothes, like on picture day. Maybe it would make it easier to change for gym class. OK, I'll get a bra, if I have to. I know you always made tough choices and did what you had to do, RBG. I guess I can too.

Dear RBG:

Today my mom took me to the store to get a bra. I couldn't believe it. There were racks and racks with all different kinds. There were pretty lace ones, ones with padding, and all different colors. Some even had princesses and other characters on them, and some had flowers or bows. They looked like a short undershirt with an elasticized bottom and matching underpants. Those didn't look too bad. Some of them were cute. I found one that I liked with a little lace on the sides by the arms and a green bow in the middle. But my mom said those wouldn't work for me because I needed something to pad me, so I don't poke through my shirts and dresses. Like I need these to be bigger? No way.

In another area, she found bras in boxes with pictures of girls on them. I didn't think they were for me because the girls in the pictures looked much older, like junior high or high school. The boxes all had numbers and letters. There were letters from AAA to C. I thought maybe it was like the grades in school, A, B, C, etc. In school, I always wanted to get A's, but I usually got B's, so I grabbed the B box out of habit. I would get more A's if it weren't for math and science. I stink at those subjects. But my mom explained that the numbers are for inches and the letters are the size of the cups. I wonder why they call them cups? They don't look like any cups we have at my house. I tried on a couple of bras in the dressing room. They were really hard to get on, so my mom helped me. I had to lean over a little, put my arms through the straps, and then she clasped it in the back. It was so tight I could barely breathe. And it was really scratchy with these wire hooks that scraped my back. The straps held me up. I felt like a puppet with someone above me pulling the strings. My mom says that's their job, to keep you up. At least it makes my posture better. I'm always getting yelled at for hunching over too much.

The straps have plastic buckles that you can make tighter or looser. After trying on a few, we found one that fit—32A. At least my mom says it fits. I think it makes me look like I have two arrows in my shirt pointing outward. The only nice thing is the bow on the front, in the middle of the boobs. It's cute, but I hate this bra. It's uncomfortable and makes my shirt look bad. I think it looks worse than before when I was just poking out. My mom says I'll get used to it. I hope

so. I wonder if you did. I bet you probably got away

with no bra because you wore that big black robe all

of the time, RBG. But why do I always have to get

used to things? Is that what life is about, not liking

something but just submitting?

Suzanne Rudd

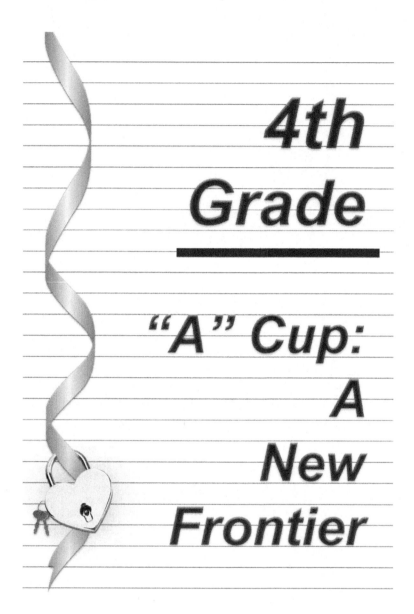

4th Grade

"A" Cup: A New Frontier

Dear RBG:

Today was the first day of school with the new bra. I had the hardest time getting it on. What a pain. It didn't seem that hard in the store, but it took me ten whole minutes this morning just to get the hooks clasped in the back by myself. My mom said I need to put it on backwards first to see the hooks and then spin it around, but I couldn't get it turned around. Then when I finally turned it around, the cups mashed up, and the straps were all wrong. And the whole time my brother was yelling at me to hurry up, so we didn't miss the bus. The more he yelled, the more I'd get distracted and the longer it took. Finally, I heard the front door slam. He left without me. I got flustered, and then I couldn't get my boobs into the cups. Everything was lopsided. This is so stupid. I'm just glad it's wintertime, so my coat covered it up and no one would notice.

I got to the bus just in time. The driver was honking, but she waited when she saw me running for the bus. Our bus stop is about a block away from our house, so I had to run fast to make it. When I got to my assigned seat, I was out of breath, but I whispered to Sandy that I had a bra on. She really didn't seem to care, but maybe she didn't know what it was. Sandy lives on the next street, and we sit on the bus together. She's a tomboy and the only girl in her family, so she mostly wears jeans, shirts, and sneakers. She says she would never be caught dead in a dress. She has an older brother and a younger brother. Her little brother is a real pain, always annoying and teasing us when we're at her house. Her older brother is just plain creepy. He always says weird stuff like "how's it going, ladies" and "are ya workin' hard or hardly workin'" when we study together. I don't know where he gets these sayings.

He tries to act cool in front of us just because he's in Jr. High. I think he's the only one who thinks he's cool. At least the other older kids in the neighborhood don't seem to think so.

My teacher is Miss Cassidy. She's so pretty. She has long black hair that she wears off her face in a ponytail. Her clothes are really nice, like the ones you see in the store windows at the mall and online. I think she looks like a model. I follow all the fashion trends with online magazines and I follow several people on social media. My mom won't let me post anything or follow any real people, but she said I can look at fashion. I especially like shoes. Mrs. Cassidy always has the cutest heels. I can't wear them yet, but I try to find the cutest shoes I can get at my age. I know there are more important things than clothes, RBG, but why can't you fight for what's right and still look good? I see you did that with your judge robe and the lace collar. I love that you personalized it.

I saw shoes that looked just like Miss Cassidy's at the mall and asked my mom if I could get them for school. She said I couldn't wear them because I'd fall off them. I have to admit, I do trip sometimes when I walk, well, a lot of the time. My mom says some girls are like that at this age because they're growing. So, I buy the nicest flats and low shoes I can find. Someday I'll be able to dress like her.

This is Miss Cassidy's first class. She graduated from college last year. She's so cool. I love to watch her when she gives us lessons. She has to wear a bra, right? All grown up ladies do, my mom says. I think she does because she is not poking through her dress like a tent. Although, her boobs don't look very big. Since I grew these things, I've become very observant of women in all shapes and sizes. I'm kind of an expert on bras now, after trying so many on. Well, if wearing a bra was going to make me pretty, cool, and grown-up like her someday, it probably couldn't be that bad.

Dear RBG:

I've been wearing this bra for ONE WHOLE WEEK. I was wrong. It's that bad. You probably already know that. You wore one forever. I have to wear this thing all day, every day. I get to take it off when I'm at home, but that's it. It's itchy and scratchy, and I hate it. It feels so weird. I've been able to cover it up pretty well. I keep my arms crossed or hold my books up to my chest when walking around, so no one will see it. And when I'm sitting, I hunch a little, and luckily my desk covers it. Although there goes my posture again. I've been able to conceal it until gym class today. We didn't dress for gym for a few days this week because of an outdoor sports tournament. It was a little cool but still OK to be outside, so we were told to dress warm for outdoor activities. But today, it rained, so we're back inside for gym. I asked Sandy to block me from the other girls again when we're getting dressed. I always run right to gym with my books after class, so I can get the end locker in the corner of the room. Then she can block me from the rest of them. It worked when we were getting dressed. But gym went long, and we were rushed to get to an assembly in the cafeteria on the other side of the school, so we didn't have a lot of time to change back into our school clothes. We had to dress fast, and Sandy couldn't block me from the other girls.

I know some of the girls saw my bra. Something was up because, during the assembly, I saw the twins, Lucy and Laura L., talking to the kids around them, looking at me, pointing, and then talking to the kids again. Their lockers were across from mine today in gym. They must have seen my bra and told everyone around them. I could see the chatter rush like a flood quickly from seat to seat, person to person, all across the bleachers to everyone in our class. Within minutes, everyone knew, boys and girls. Gossip in grade school is like a tsunami—it can't be held back even with that Hoover Dam we learned about in Nevada. It always leaks out right away or bursts.

I'm not paranoid, really. I know it's true because later that day, boys kept coming up to me during recess, grabbing the bra strap on my back, and snapping it like a slingshot, even through my light jacket. Boy, that hurt. I yelled something at them. I can't even remember what. They laughed and ran away. Dumb boys! After it happened a couple of times, I played jump rope so I didn't have to deal with them. No room for those idiots in Double Dutch.

Those twins are always out to get me. I compete against them all the time in choir for solos and spots in voice contests. I mean, it's not like I get everything—they beat me out a lot. And there are two of them. I win some, and each of them wins some. They're in the cheerleader group. They're so snooty. I don't think of them as my arch nemeses or anything, but maybe just frenemies. It's game on now. I know you never let the haters get to you, RBG, but I guess I do.

Dear RBG:

This is a nightmare. For three whole days, they've been harassing me on the playground. Boys keep coming up and snapping my bra strap. And when I turn around to yell at them, another boy in back of me, snaps it again. Then they laugh, and the mean girls laugh and point. It really hurts on my back—a lot. Good thing I'm not the crying type because it's enough to make most people cry. I'm mad, embarrassed, and frustrated. I mean really, grow up already. What's the big deal? Boys can be really stupid. So can girls.

Sandy and a couple of other friends came to my rescue and pulled me away for a game. I almost wish the cold winter weather would come sooner than later. There's no way they could snap the strap through my big winter coat.

I know they're trying to help, but my friends don't get what I'm going through. They tell me not to worry about it and just shrug it off, but it was a big deal to me.

I even told my mom, and she said they would forget about it, eventually. "Something new and different is always going to be scoffed at," she said. "They're uneasy at something new, so they lash out and try to make fun of it." She says it'll pass.

Even my wise grandma told me to turn the other cheek when I went to her for help. She threw a few of her "crosses to bear" sayings at me, and that was that.

I get it—they're morons, as my dad always says. He calls everyone either a moron or an idiot. But seriously, when will this stop? Every day at school is torture. It's distracting me during classes. I keep seeing kids drawing pictures and passing them when the teacher isn't looking. When we're not in class, people giggle and whisper to each other, always looking and pointing at me. Gym continues to be difficult too. We're all indoors now because it's colder. The boys keep chasing me around, trying to snap my back bra strap and some of the girls keep laughing. One of these days I'm going to crack and haul off and belt one of them. I'm really tempted. Especially Mark C. I know I'm not supposed to, but I'm either going to strike soon or break down. You never backed down from a fight, RBG, but I think you knew how hard it is to be the targeted bullseye all the time. It's not easy.

My mom says boys this age always tease girls they like. I don't know about that, but if it's true, I wish they'd like me less. My back is getting black and blue. And I'm so sick of this. Is this another thing I have to get used to?

My friends yell at them too and help me try to evade them altogether. I really appreciate them. My friends are the only thing keeping me from going berserk!

Dear RBG:

After a couple of weeks, the teasing decreased to just snickers and points when they saw me in the hall or at lunch. I wish every day for someone else to get a bra and take some of the heat off of me. Or maybe something else could happen for them to buzz

39

about. Maybe someone could wear something hideous or get a bad haircut. I don't want anyone else to have to endure this, but I'm thinking of a "spread the wealth" type idea. I think we learned something like that in social studies.

Of course, my real friends keep telling me to ignore them. That's easy for them to say. No one's mocking them. And my mom and grandma keep saying it'll pass.

"New is new, different is different, and anything new and different takes a little time for anyone to get used to," my grandma told me. That's not one of her best sayings. I hope when I'm a grandma, I'll have better things to say.

"Kids tease when they don't understand," my mom said. "And boys your age are just starting to notice girls. You're all starting to develop into women; there's a lot of strange information coming at you all at once. It's easier to make fun than to deal with the reality that you're all growing and changing."

It's not like they've never seen a bra or breasts—underclothes, of course. There are developed women on the street, in stores, on TV, online, in movies, everywhere. But I guess not girls at their school and not in fourth grade.

I don't think I'll talk about it to my friends or family anymore. They mean well, but explanations and excuses for their behavior don't make it any easier if you are the target. And it doesn't fix it, either. I'm wasting my breath.

Dear RBG:

I guess I'm getting used to everything. I can finally put the bra on and not miss the bus, and things are simmering down in school. I guess my bra is yesterday's news, just like everyone said.

Then today, Missy K. got a bra. Hurrah! Missy K. and I were not good friends or anything. We were friends in K-3, but as you get older, people start to drift into different friend circles. She wasn't even in my class this year. You hang around with people in your class a lot, so most of the time, you hang out with your friend circle within your class. I think it's like a giant Venn Diagram. We just learned about that in science class. It's not science, but it seems to connect. Your class is one circle, and other classes are other circles. School groups like choir, band, art, and sports may cause the different class circles to intersect. Your core friend group changes based on what circles you are in. That's just the way it works in school.

I saw Missy K.'s bra in gym class today. So did the other girls. You would think by now they would be over it. But no, they pointed and snickered, just like with me. I didn't laugh. I felt bad for her. I knew that feeling very well. She's a little prissy, full of herself, and very stuck up. So, she just acted like she didn't hear them or didn't care. But I knew. She cared.

I have to admit, RBG, it felt a little good to have another target for them to aim at. I know you would've protected and stuck up for her, but I just couldn't. I didn't want them to focus on me again. I feel bad. I'm not strong enough to fight them. I have too many scars.

Dear RBG:

It probably serves me right, but it turns out Missy K. didn't take the heat off of me, as I expected. It just started the whole thing up again. And this time, there were two girls to torment. Boys are unpredictable sometimes—and still stupid. Seriously, when will more girls start getting bras, so it's no longer a novelty.

But I thought of what you would've done, RBG, and I went to Missy in choir to tell her that I know how she feels. She's not at my recess, so choir and gym were the only times I saw her. I guess I just wanted to see if she wanted to talk about it, or if she wanted to have an alliance in the locker room for our mutual protection. I figured if more of us banded together, maybe we could overcome the mean girls and snuff out the snickers. You would've done that, RBG.

I told her I see the girls giggling and boys pointing and that they did it to me too, when I started wearing a bra. I said they're stupid and that there's nothing wrong with wearing a bra. And I told her if she ever wanted to talk, we could talk after choir. My grandma says misery loves company. Right? But her reaction really surprised me.

"I don't know what you are talking about. No one makes fun of me!" she barked at me. She flipped her hair and walked across the room.

That girl is in serious denial. I tried, RBG. But at least she heard that someone else has the same problem and feels bad about it. Maybe that'll help.

Dear RBG:

Yesterday was Valentine's Day at school. I was up late filling out cards for every single person in my class. That's the rule, so no one feels bad. We have to give a card to everyone—even the mean girls, haters, dumb boys, teasers, and yes, even frenemies. I decided to do the "turn the other cheek" thing my grandma always talks about, and I asked my mom to buy me some candy to put on each card. I taped a piece of candy to every Valentine. Although I did put the best candy on Valentines for the people I like and put the candy I don't like on the cards for people I

45

don't like. But it's still candy, right? It made me feel a little better anyway.

At the end of the day, this boy in my class, Mikey P., gave me a small box of chocolate candies in a heart-shaped box with a card. I couldn't believe it. I didn't know what to say. I held back a giggle and just smiled and said thank you. I'm pretty sure my face turned red. It was really nice to get something so special. I don't think anyone else did.

He's cute. Some of the other girls like him too. I definitely got glares from Lisa M. and Robin S. I think they're mad he gave it to me and not them. When we were waiting for the bus on the playground, I read the card.

"To: Katie R. From: Mikey P. I like you and Missy K. from choir, but your box of candy is bigger."

I don't know if I like-like him that way, or any boy for that matter. I don't know if Missy K. likes him too. I don't know how I feel about being part of a love triangle. I saw that on TV once. Then I thought of the connection between Missy K. and me. The only girls in school with a bra both get candy from this boy? But he was a nice boy. He was kind of shy and never snapped my bra strap or laughed and pointed at me, like many of the other boys. Maybe this "bra thing" does have its advantages. Maybe it makes us both seem prettier? Nah.

But you'll never guess what happened, RBG? Missy K. came up to me and smiled and said. "I see you got chocolates too. Now we have two things in common. Don't worry, I'm not ready for boys yet. He's all yours." I told her I wasn't either, and we both laughed. I think we're making progress with her, RBG. I think you legal eagles call that an olive branch.

Dear RBG:

We're practicing for our final choir performance of the year. My choir director, Mr. Wardman, gets so excited about his pageants, as he calls them. We're doing a big performance with all songs about America. He even wrote a song about the 50 states, where everyone in choir dresses up like someone from each state and says something. I'm excited. We wrote the two states we wanted on paper and turned it in to him. He chose if there were any duplicates. I wrote Georgia and Hawaii.

I was thinking about the costumes. I'd been to Hawaii once on vacation and had a grass hula skirt and lei and some flowered wrist bracelets and flowers for my hair, so that would be pretty easy. And my mom had a wide pink hat and long dress and parasol from her prom. I guess they did theme proms back then because that's not what I see for prom wear now. She wore it for a Halloween costume, and now it does fit me, as I am her height now, so that could work for a southern belle.

I ended up with Georgia, so that was OK. Missy K. got Hawaii. She'd been there on vacation too and had the same costume. It looked nice, especially all the flowers she put in her long curly dark hair. But for some reason, she wore a bikini top for the costume. Would you have worn a bikini top in the fourth grade if you were one of only two girls who had boobs and wore a bra, RBG? I wouldn't, and I'm one of those girls. Way to put a big target right on your chest. I don't know what she was thinking. And yes, the first dress rehearsal, the giggles, laughs, pointing, and snickering started at the beginning of rehearsal and didn't stop.

Mr. Wardman didn't seem to notice or pay attention. He's very focused on the music and choreography, so a lot gets by him in class. Plus he's gay, so he probably didn't realize the costume was a little old for her, let's say. I felt really bad for her, but secretly I was relieved that I dodged a bullet. That could have been me. She held it together and didn't cry, but since I was next to her in alphabetical state order, I tried to help by blocking her chest with my parasol and hat as much as I could. I think it helped a little. Missy smiled at me. I know she was grateful. For the performance, she wore a tank top instead. The bikini looked nice, but it's just not worth the hassle.

Suzanne Rudd

5th Grade

"B" Cup Seriously – They're getting bigger?

Dear RBG:

Sorry I didn't write much this summer. I was too busy. I stayed at my aunt and uncle's house in the country all summer to help take care of their new twin boys. I like staying with them. It's so different from my home. There's always music on in their house, and they're constantly singing and dancing. They live out in the middle of nowhere, so we were going on hikes, to the beach, and camping all summer long.

They let me do whatever I want. My aunt says a girl can't grow into a woman unless she's given freedom to make her own choices. You would've liked them, RBG. I think they're your kind of people. And my aunt says I didn't even have to wear a bra if I didn't want to. And I <u>didn't</u>. It was wonderful. All summer, no bra and no one to tease me. I felt so open and free.

This week I started school and had to put a bra back on. But over the summer, my boobs kept growing. Three months without a bra, and I didn't even know it happened. My mom took me back to the store, and now I need a bigger size—a "B" cup. I know dealt with much worse in your life, but for me, this is a personal terror. I have only had these things for one year! Are they supposed to grow every year? I don't think I can handle that. By the time I get a driver's license, I won't fit behind the steering wheel.

Dear RBG:

I started fifth grade this week. There are some new kids in the class, along with some of the same ones. Sandy has a different homeroom now - that stinks. But since we switch teachers and classrooms now all year, I'm hoping we'll be together for maybe lunch or gym. And no more recess! That's a very good thing. Most kids are mad about it, but it saves me from a black-and-blue back. Who knows, maybe the kids will have grown up a little over the summer.

Unfortunately, while things kept changing for me, it didn't seem to happen to everyone. I thought I bloomed early, and everyone else would catch up by now. Like with height, I was in the middle row instead of the back row in this year's class picture. Wouldn't you think more girls would have "blossomed" over the summer? No such luck. Many girls still don't wear a bra, and now that mine grew again, they were even more noticeable. Plus, they really started getting in the way.

Gym class, as always, was a real pain. It started with the usual stares that still took place in the locker room. Sandy and I are in gym together, thank goodness, and so is Missy. We have an alliance now since I helped her last year. The locker room changing "blocking" plan works much better with more girls. But now, we're mixed with the boys for every class AND playing contact sports. Fun, huh?

The horror started when the teacher wanted to "check out the talent" as he called it. Our gym teacher, Mr. Marek, is a very tall and skinny man with big, thick glasses. And even though he's an adult, he wears tube socks all the way up to his knees. Maybe that's because he wears shorts and teaches P.E., but none of the boys wear them that high, only girls. He's very nice. He always smiles at everyone, but he makes strange jokes and says things that no one understands. And I don't think he remembers names because he calls all the boys "sport" and all the girls "missy." There are two girls named Missy in the class, so that's confusing. I think Mr. Marek is considered a little geeky. Is that mean to say?

Since my growth spurt last year, I have pretty long legs and can run fast. And, I admit it; I was showing off a little. One time we were running laps around the gym track, and I didn't realize that they were bouncing up and down—a lot. One very obnoxious boy, Kurt T., pointed it out, and the laughing spread like the plague, fast and furious. At first, I didn't know they were laughing at me. But then my new friend Brittany told me what they were laughing about. She overheard them talking. I was humiliated and ran into the girl's locker room. I didn't cry, though. I will never cry and give them the satisfaction.

From the first snickering last year, I promised myself I would never cry or let them see me upset. I usually yell at the hecklers, which probably shows I'm upset, now that I think about it. But I always try to use clever words and arguments to deflect any teasing and humiliate them instead. I thought of you, RBG. You always argued your way out of problems. And since I read a lot of books and know a lot of big words, I can argue pretty well. Maybe I will make a good lawyer. But now I have a reputation as being too tough and having a big mouth. So wrong.

Dear RBG:

Gym just keeps getting worse. It's like daily torture. The boys and some of the girls wait every day for it to happen. Bounce. Bounce. Bounce. I tried to fold my arms across my chest to keep them down, but sports require a lot of movement, and sometimes I need to use my hands too. It didn't work.

I couldn't stop running in gym, as most sports require it, but I wasn't about to go through that agony every day. So, I took an Ace bandage from the medicine cabinet at home. My dad used it once when he hurt his leg in softball, sliding into base. Before we changed into our gym uniforms, I quickly wrapped the bandage around my chest a couple of times to keep them down. I got the idea from a book I read. It said they used Ace bandages in the filming of *Wizard of Oz* to keep sixteen-year-old Judy Garland from looking too old, as the character in the book was supposed to be a younger girl who had not developed.

That worked for a while, but it was very uncomfortable and made me sweat a lot. And the sweat gave me red marks under my boobs where my bra strap rubbed against my skin. It itched and hurt, but at least it kept the hyenas from laughing and made gym class a little easier. I guess crisis averted, for now.

Dear RBG:

Whoever invented gym in schools, or P.E., as Mr. Marek calls it, must have been a miserable person who wanted to torment children. Actually, I looked it up on Wikipedia. No one person invented P.E. So, darn, no one to blame.

Our teacher, Mr. Marek, likes a lot of contact sports. This is the first year we're in class with the boys, and he wants the girls to compete at the same level. That's what he said anyway. I appreciate his confidence, but for the first time, I really didn't want to be treated equally. I know that's bad to say, but I really hate gym. For the greater good, I guess I have to suck it up. Equality all the time, every time!

Dodgeball is Mr. Marek's favorite sport in class. Especially in the winter, it occupies the entire class indoors, so it makes sense. I don't know if you played this game when you were a kid, RBG, but it's a horrible game. The whole object of the game is to deliberately aim the ball and directly bean someone on the other team. I looked dodgeball up on Wikipedia too. It began as an Africa war game where people threw rocks at each other in an attempt to injure their opponents. It was a form of training for battle. People actually died. Definitely not a kid's game.

Missionaries brought the idea back to England and turned it into a game with a rubber ball to be less brutal. It was very popular in colleges to teach agility. Then Phillip Ferguson brought it to the US. Finally, someone to blame! Curse you, Phillip Ferguson.

Even though we use rubber balls instead of rocks, dodgeball was still brutal. Somehow mostly boys and some girls decided it was a free-for-all and went on a beaning spree to knock down any kid in their wake. Even though they were not supposed to hit hard or hit in the face, one after another, every day slower and less athletic kids in school were victims of the daily carnage of this sadistic sport.

For me, this game created a whole other set of issues. One day, this jerky kid Adam L. decided that the art of aiming to hit people wasn't challenging enough, so he set out to target not only me but my chest, in particular, as a big bullseye.

I wasn't great at the game…or a lot of sports for that matter. I didn't have good aim, so I was picked toward the last for teams and usually one of the first out of the game. That helped, but my boobs were the perfect target. Unfortunately, I never saw it coming until the last minute. That was my fatal error. He got close enough to me and slammed that ball directly at my chest. It really hurt. I went down in a lot of pain, but again, I just yelled something, and they just laughed.

As dodgeball was a frequent occurrence at my school, it didn't take long for the other boys to figure this out and join in the "fun" and make my boobs their target too. The most I could do was stay in the back, hide behind other kids, or turn around or on the side, so they hit me elsewhere. I know it's not good sportsmanship, but I admit, I would turn my back and deliberately try to get hit first and go out. Stupid boys, stupid game! I'm like one of those moving ducks in a carnival shooting gallery game.

Dear RBG:

Science is NOT my favorite subject. This year it's getting a little more challenging. My teacher is Mrs. Burns. She's very strict, very stern, and very small. I tower over her, she has to be about four-and-a-half-feet tall. But what she lacks in height, she makes up for with her booming voice. Going to her class is like being in the army. Everything is regimented. Relaxing or mistakes are not tolerated. I think everyone in the class is afraid of her and I think she likes it that way.

I'm having a little trouble in her class, and she keeps yelling at me. I'm thankful she doesn't have a weapon. I got in trouble twice last week. I asked someone next to me about a couple of words on the board. We're seated in class alphabetically by last name. As an "R," I'm in the second to the back row. Sometimes I can't see all the words on the board clearly. When I quietly asked my neighbor what the word was, she immediately shouted at me. She must have sonar or superhuman hearing. One little question got me a warning. Three warnings, and I get an "F" in the class.

The next warning was because I couldn't see through the microscope in our lab. We partnered up to make observations and identifications through the microscope and take notes. I tried the full magnification, but I just couldn't see the microscope slide clearly. So, I asked my lab partner if I could write all the notes, and she could identify and describe the slide. I really thought I was getting the raw end of the stick. I had to write out all the notes, observations, and definitions and write the report for the team. I like to write, so I didn't mind. My partner Dawn was glad as she didn't like to write, but Mrs. Burns didn't see it that way.

"Miss Reed," she barked. "Do you think you can skip out on the work in this class and just skate by on your partner's hard work?"

"No, Mrs. Burns," I explained. "But I'm having a hard time seeing through the microscope, so Dawn is doing the observations and identification, and I'll write all the notes and create the report, which will take more time."

"Your problem is not my problem," she warned. "If you can't do the work, you will fail this lab."

So, Dawn helped me, and I faked it. Boy, Mrs. Burns is mean.

I don't understand why I can't see. I just passed a vision test at school. But, then again, those are pretty easy to pass. They only have one device to look into and have the whole class line up in front of it, and one by one, recite the same letters, as everyone in the class listens. Since everyone lines up in alphabetical order, I was toward the end of the line. By the time they reached me, I probably remembered the letters instead of seeing them.

After a few weeks of struggling to read the board in a few classes, my mom took me to the eye doctor. And you guessed it—I need glasses! Just another thing to make me stand out as a target of ridicule ($5 word). I could almost hear them taunting "four-eyes" as I tried on glasses in the doctor's office. I heard them call a kid that once. My mom said I could maybe get contacts next year, but for now, I have to wear these glasses. She said it wouldn't be that bad.

She doesn't know. I know you wore glasses, RGB. I wonder if you wore them when you were a kid. My grandma says only studious children wear glasses— like it's some prize. Be smart and be a target. Pray for me.

Dear RBG:

Things are looking up. I was in the school library the other day and talked to the librarian, Miss Appleton. I read a lot, so I'm in there all the time. She said she needs someone to work in there during fourth period. That's my gym class period! I consider her a friend, so I told her what was happening in gym class. Believe it or not, she knows exactly how I feel. She was teased as a kid for being a little overweight. Before this happened to me, I never realized how many kids get laughed at for nothing. It doesn't make any sense. Why do kids do that? How does it affect them if someone is tall, skinny or fat, wears old clothes, has glasses or braces, or has big boobs? Isn't being a kid hard enough with school pressures and all the puberty stuff?

Miss Appleton said she would talk to the principal about getting me out of gym. She is a lady too and has a sympathetic ear. At least that is what Miss Appleton said. I couldn't believe it—NO MORE GYM CLASS!! The principal said she could make an exception since I was on the park district tennis team. I guess it pays to have friends in high places. RBG, you probably knew that; you were on the highest court in the US. You probably had friends in a lot of high places. Now that I know it can be done, I'm making it my personal mission to get out of gym whenever and however I can for the rest of my school life.

Dear RBG:

Fifth grade may be a better year. For the first time, we get to change classes and teachers four times a day. So, I'm meeting new kids. It's a pretty big school, and with all the new homes being built, people are moving here all the time. And it turns out that a few kids wear glasses, so maybe I will survive that after all.

I met this new girl, Dani. She wears glasses too. She just moved here from Puerto Rico. Her father is an engineer for the government, and she moves around a lot. She's very sweet and quiet. She doesn't talk because she has a pretty bad stutter. It's no big deal—I can understand her if I'm patient and really listen to her. I feel bad. It must be hard for her, especially moving to new schools all the time. I know how it feels to be teased for something that's not your fault. She can't help that she stutters. So what? I still just don't get why some kids spend all their time being mean to other kids.

The other day, I saw some boys making fun of her when I met her for lunch. Four of them backed her into a corner and imitated her stuttering, then laughed. She was ready to cry, so I yelled at them and called them Neanderthals. It's in my big words book, a $20 word. They just got confused and left. They don't know what to say. Ha! Victory, for now at least. I'm sticking with her. Sandy protected me last year, and I'm glad to help someone else out. We're good friends. It feels good to help others, RBG. I bet that's how you felt all the time.

Dear RBG:

Fifth grade is better than fourth grade. You learn more challenging things, which I like. And I like having different teachers and changing rooms. It's interesting. Some teachers are good and some are not great. My social studies teacher, Mrs. Hannibal, is an older lady—like a grandma or maybe even a great-grandma. I bet she's been teaching forever. She keeps falling asleep in class. She tells us to read the chapter, and then she's out for the count. It gets a little rowdy because everyone just messes around and talks. Some kids throw paper footballs to each other and run in the classroom. Others take out there phones and go on social media. I guess some kids are allowed even at this age. She can't hear anything because she snores—really loud. It's funny, but it can get out of hand. And no one learns anything. I have to use my library time to read the book chapters. I don't know why she's still teaching.

My favorite class is English. We're reading some classic novels, as it's an advanced class. I thought smarter students would be more serious and less juvenile ($10 word). My teacher, Mrs. Lewis, is nice. I liked the class a lot at first because it's books. What's not to love? But now I dread it. Mrs. Lewis started wearing white blouses every day. The problem is she wears dark-colored bras and you can see the bra right through her shirt, especially when she stands in front of the windows in the room. I don't think she knows. But yes, you guessed it, now that this started, the Neanderthals, as I now call them, are giggling again. They must have pea brains. Any little thing that has to do with boobs or bras has them laughing like hyenas, and, of course, they take it out on me. "What color is yours?" they say. Dummies! Will it ever stop? It's a shame because English is my favorite subject and now it's my worst class.

Dear RBG:

I love working at the library. Since I'm a prolific reader ($15 word), Miss Appleton gives me all the books she wants to buy for the library to read, and then she asks for my opinion. With a whole hour during the day, plus my nighttime reading, I'm going through a lot of books. I love it.

Miss Appleton is great. I can talk to her about anything. I stopped telling my mom and grandma any of this stuff because all they do is give me old sayings and excuses. They just don't get it. She listens and understands because she went through it too. This week she gave me a psychology book about bullying. She said it might be too advanced for some of the kids in the school, but she wanted me to read it and let her know what I thought.

There are a lot of big words, so yes, some of these dumb-dumbs wouldn't get it. But it's interesting. It gives many reasons why kids are mean and bully others. The book says they crave attention from other kids, parents, and teachers. Some of them don't feel good about themselves and try to hurt other kids to push up their self-esteem and become popular with other kids or stay at the top of their clique group. It also says that some kids who bully feel they don't have control because parents or older brothers and sisters bully them. Sometimes, they are prejudiced by what they hear at home and want to make their parents proud that they are fixing the world. That's why they bully kids who are different than them. The book says that most kids are not evil or malicious (that's $25 word), even if their behavior is bad. I'm surprised. Nowhere did it say that they're simply stupid.

I looked it up online to make sure. One article says some bullies are actually smart, and school is not challenging enough, so they get bored and lash out at other kids for excitement. I guess it explains some things, but it still doesn't make it right. Why should they make me or anyone else a target because of their problems? Maybe my grandma is right—turn the other cheek and walk in their shoes, etc. I will try to think of their issues, but I just want to fight back—with words, of course. Not fists.

Dear RBG:

Summer was great. I spent the summer at my aunt's house again this year, and I met a new friend down the street. Her name is Susan, but everyone calls her Suz. It fits her. She's bubbly like soapsuds. She's the youngest and the only girl in a family with four boys. I still had plenty of babysitting duties with the twins and fun trips with my aunt antiquing and shopping, but it was nice to have a friend for the summer to do girl things. We spent a lot of time at the beach, and Suz even asked me to a beach party for her birthday. A lot of boys were invited, so my aunt bought me a new swimsuit—a bikini.

We went to the store, and I tried on a bunch of suits. What a pain that was. There were a lot of cute suits, but I couldn't get one to fit. Because of my boobs, if the bottoms fit, the top was too small, and if the top fit, the bottoms were too big. My aunt was great though, so patient. She looked online and found a store that sold separates. I got different sizes for the top and bottom. Everything fit great.

Suz is two years older than me. For her thirteenth birthday, her mom let her have boys at her beach party. And her brothers were there and brought some of their older friends. None of them knew me or how old I was. It was fun but weird for me. With the new bikini and my developing figure, I looked a little older than I am. Plus, I had a great tan from being outside all summer, and I stopped wearing my hair in ponytails and braids and let my long blonde hair hang down. For the first time, I wasn't getting teased for the way I looked. I was getting positive attention. Boys would come over and talk to me and ask me to go for a swim and play games. I felt awkward. I didn't know what to say to older boys. I don't even like boys yet. I like boys online and in magazines and have quite a few posters on my wall at home of TV personalities, movie stars, and singers. All girls do. But I didn't know what to do with this attention. So, I stuck to Suz like glue.

I did have a little embarrassing accident though. I guess I haven't grown out of my clutsy phase all the way. We played beach volleyball. It was fun. Usually I hate sports, but it seemed fun, and everyone was having a good time. I played in gym before, but that's it. Everyone was really nice though, so I let my guard down and got into the game. That's when it happened. I reached for a ball and fell face down in the sand. I was ashamed. I felt like a clod. But to my surprise, no one was laughing. I was relieved, so I got up and started wiping off the sand.

But I didn't realize that when I fell, my boob fell out of my bikini top. Not totally, thank goodness, but enough. I was mortified ($20 word). I don't know if anyone noticed, so quickly I said I had to rinse off and ran into the bathroom to readjust. I hoped maybe the sand-covered everything, or maybe no one paid attention. I couldn't take the chance. After I washed off, I told Suz I hurt my knee and had to go home. Once I got home, I told my aunt what happened. I didn't cry, but I was close. My aunt pointed out that I didn't really know any of those kids and probably would never see them again. That makes me feel better. I wonder if you ever had anything happen to you like that, RBG?

Suzanne Rudd

.

6th Grade

"C" Cup: Not Again – Bigger?

Dear RBG:

I'm in sixth grade now, and you guessed it—
after another no-bra summer, I grew another size
again. I first noticed it when none of my button-up
shirts fit. There are big gaps between the buttons.
When I went school shopping, I figured I just wouldn't
buy any button-up shirts. But every time I tried shirts
or dresses on, I saw bulges coming out of my bra in
the middle, side, and bottom. My mom said it was
time to get another bra. So, we went bra shopping
again. I really hope this is it. I haven't grown taller in
two years, so maybe I have peaked there too? I don't
want to get new bras every year. The only good part
is that the selection is a little better in this size. There
were many more colors and styles. I got a couple of
cute pink and blue lacy ones, but only light colors. I
remembered about Mrs. Lewis last year. No white
shirts and no dark bras. No way. Why ask for it?

Dear RBG:

I'm kind of excited about sixth grade. In my school, this is the start of junior high. A new building and even more kids fed from three different middle schools. It's the same town, so a lot of kids know each other from sports and park district activities. I know a few girls from the dance studio and the park district tennis team, but it was a new beginning.

The building is three stories, so you walk up and down stairs to get to some classes. I had to walk fast and even run sometimes to get to class on time.

My grandma says junior high is a rite of passage for kids. "It's like training wheels for a social life." The summer taught me a little of that. Boys and girls are noticing each other more, I guess. But there's still a lot of giggling. "Giddy," my mom calls it.

Everything's changing again. I first noticed it in swimming class. My library job got me out of gym, but

I had to take a swimming class for the first few weeks of school. My mom says the school wanted everyone to be able to swim so no one would drown. Of course, that's important and all, but I'm a great swimmer. I swim at the beach and the lake all the time. My brother and I had to swim two laps of the pool when I was eleven, so we could go on paddleboats by ourselves. My mom says it's a rule because not everyone can swim.

In swimming class, everyone has to wear the same swimsuits. I just don't understand why we have to all match all the time. It's not like we were playing another team or anything. But of course, I had to get a new swimsuit. It looks just like the ones I saw the Olympic swimmers wore on TV last summer. It was a dark, ugly color with a high neck and no design at all. And it didn't have any bra cups or padding at the chest. When I tried it on at home, let's just say, things stuck out. I know this is going to be another nightmare. The first week was horrible. This swimsuit is a new form of torture. The boys are snickering, and some of the girls are giggling. But this time, they're not just laughing at me. Some girls are still flat, but there are a few girls who developed over the summer. And those swimsuits made even an "A" cup stick out. Maybe more misery loves more company?

Our swim teacher, Mr. Connelly, is an older Irish man with a thick accent. He says he never taught girls before and really didn't want them now. He loses his temper a lot, mostly at the boys, with all the giggling and snickering. He says everyone is "acting the maggot" and tells a group of boys, "May the cat eat you, and may the devil eat the cat." I have no idea what any of those things mean, and neither do any of the other kids, but things settle down a little when he yells. He's a big man, so when he yells, everyone's a little afraid. When he isn't shouting, he sounds like the leprechaun on the "Lucky Charms" cereal commercial. That's funny.

After the first week, two girls told Mr. Connelly they had their period and couldn't swim for at least a week. So, I told him I had my period too. It's a little lie. I didn't have my period then, but I figure it was one less week of swimming, changing into that horrible suit, and then going back to class with wet hair. That's fine with me. He just shook his head and muttered, "Sure fed, do it," and handed us passes to study hall. I couldn't make out what he said, so I looked it up. It's "chuirfeadh as duit." In Celtic, it means annoying person.

I think he forgot about us. We've been in study hall for three weeks. We all talked after the week was over and decided to keep going to study hall. There were different teachers for study hall all the time, and

Diary of a 6th Grade "c" Cup

other kids were coming in and out every day, so I think we got lost in the shuffle. Most of the teachers just read the newspaper or worked on the computer anyway. I think some of them play games on the computer because I heard some game music one time. They must have learned their lesson because now the volume is always turned down. If no one tells us to go back to swimming, we aren't going to say anything.

Dear RBG:

Sixth grade is different. It's like a bridge from middle school to jr. high—stuck in between kid and teen. With no gym or swimming, there's definitely less teasing by boys. Thank goodness. But something I didn't expect recently hit me like a ton of bricks. Now my problem is other girls. It's strange. Our bodies are all changing, and you'd think we would be on the same side, right? Like a sisterhood. But now I see how jealous, catty, and hurtful girls can be when you have something they want. My mom says, "Jealousy is the best form of flattery." I don't understand why she always has an excuse for the bad behavior of others. And actually, I don't think she's right. It doesn't make sense that kids who like or envy me would create a hurricane-like wall of hate towards me. What did I do?

Last weekend I went to my first slumber party—not just an overnight at a friend's house; an actual birthday slumber party. I was so excited. I hear so many girls talk about them on Monday mornings in homeroom. They say they dance in their pajamas all night, play fun games and eat pizza, chocolate, candy, chips, and cans of soda all night! Since the object is to stay up all night, caffeine and lots of it is a requirement. And no moms are there to say you can't. Moms always say if you eat junk food, you'll get fat or break out in pimples. It's complete freedom. A girl in my science class, Karen L., invited all the girls in the class, fifteen of us, for her birthday.

Everything I heard was true. There was a huge spread on the table of every snack and treat you could think of. I have never seen so many different kinds of candy and chips in one place, except on Halloween. She even had a chocolate fountain with marshmallows, strawberries, apples, cookies, and graham crackers to dip and drench with chocolate. It was a complete mess, but it tasted great. There was a whole cooler with cans of sodas, lemonade, and other drinks. And there were several pizzas with all kinds of toppings, so everyone had a choice. I never saw anything like it before. It was kid heaven.

Everyone was dancing and singing to music, pretending to be rock stars by singing into hairbrushes or whatever was around. Karen had big aluminum foil silver stars placed all over the walls in her basement and had a disco ball in the middle of the room. When she turned the lights off, everything sparkled like diamonds with different color lights that bounced with the music. It was so much fun.

Later in the night, everyone calmed down a little, and Karen said it was time to change into pajamas. I dreaded this part. Changing in front of other girls has always been a nightmare for me, but this was worse. The uniform for the night was pajamas and no bra. Well, at least we weren't jumping around and dancing anymore, that part of the slumber urban myth was wrong.

This year, a lot of girls wore some kind of bra, even if it was more of an undershirt. And some girls even wore a padded bra or wore a size bigger than they needed and stuffed tissue paper or socks in them to appear larger than they were. But with pajamas and no bra, all truths were revealed. I enjoyed my all-natural summers, but this was a little different. I went to school with these girls every day, and it was all out there. That's when girls started looking around, comparing themselves to each other, and the stares, pointing, and whispering started. At least boys were honest about teasing, stupid, but direct. They came right out with their insults and name-calling. But girls are like lions stalking their prey with their harassment—sneaky and stealthy. They don't come out and say anything to your face. They whisper, point, and laugh to each other secretly, but close enough to ensure their victim is within earshot and just loud enough so you can hear. That's no accident.

Thankfully the games started right away. Some of the games were fun. They had a *Ouija* board and tried to contact the dead. A *Ouija* board was the chosen tool as a bridge to the other side. I read about these in a book about magician Harry Houdini. His wife held a séance every Halloween on the anniversary of this death for ten years to communicate with him from the great beyond. It never worked. This didn't either. And this version was just a plastic board game. There were even cards and dice. But all the girls got into the spirit (lol). Karen explained the game and said we all had to be quiet to hear the ghosts communicate with us. Everyone would scream when we heard any little creak or sound. In a basement, there are a lot of sounds, from water swishing to furnaces and pumps turning on. It was a silly game, but it was fun.

Another game was called "light as a feather, stiff as a board." I'm not sure what the connection is between young girls and the occult, but I think it's just a copycat. One girl has it at her party and so on and so on. In this game, girls take turns lying down with the other girls kneeling around them. Each girl puts two fingers from each hand under the girl on the floor. Then one girl holds something over the one on the floor to hypnotize her in a trance. The idea is when in a trance, she is so light that we can all lift her with just four fingers each. It never works, of course, but some girls really pretend to be hypnotized and claim afterward that they don't remember anything. It's expected and makes the game more fun, so they act as if they were in a trance. That was a blast.

Another game was called "Truth or Dare." You probably played this game before, RBG, I think everyone did at one time in their life. Everyone sits in a circle and uses a bottle as a selecting device. The first person the bottle points to asks a question of the next person the bottle chooses. The questions are mostly silly, like, "What do you think of this boy?" or,

"Do you like that boy?" or, "Which movie or rock star would you kiss or marry?" The dares were mindless things like sing a song, do a certain dance, or run up the basement stairs and shout something to Karen's parents. But then someone asked, "Who have you kissed?" to Kathy M., a shy girl. It was an obvious setup because then they made fun of her when she didn't answer. And then the next girl did the same thing, but this girl answered. She saw what happened to Kathy. I don't think many girls have kissed anyone yet. After all, it was the sixth grade. I guess some girls made it up, so they wouldn't be teased. And some didn't want to admit they liked someone. That gossip can easily get back to that boy. It was obvious Kathy was embarrassed and upset, as were the others who told the truth. I thought that was wrong and told them to stop. Boy that was a mistake. On my next turn, things went downhill fast.

I wanted to shut them up, so I choose "dare."
I'm still not sure if this dare was chosen just for me or
because of me. Either way, it made things worse. The
dare was to take my bra and put it in the freezer, and I
couldn't take it out until I got dressed in the morning.
That way it was all frozen cold and stiff. It was a
strange idea. I don't know who came up with this. It
was stupid at best and maniacal ($25 word) at worst.
But I was the first. I didn't want to, but what choice did
I have. Everyone was watching me take my bra from
my bag. I grabbed it in my hand, walked over to the
bar refrigerator they had in the basement, threw it in
the freezer, and shut the door fast. Me and my big
mouth!

After that, every "dare" was to put their bra in
the freezer. Some of the girls didn't have a bra, which
was awkward for them too. I watched as the other

girls who had bras put them into the freezer and saw the looks I got when they came back.

RBG, imagine a pile of bras in a freezer. My bra definitely stood out on a one-to-one basis or even a ten-to-one basis. It was like comparing a Chihuahua to a Great Dane. They're both dogs, but the size difference is noticeable. I don't think I hold the *Guinness Book of World Records* for being a sixth-grade "C cup." But even though many girls have developed some, most girls wanted bigger boobs or even some boobs. I think the next time I go to a slumber party maybe I won't wear a bra just to avoid that inevitability. I don't know. Sometimes it doesn't pay to fight. I hate to say that to you, RBG. You never backed away, but I did and got burned.

Dear RBG:

I don't know if you ever heard the saying "What happens somewhere stays there." Well, I found the exception to the rule – or should I say it found me. I didn't give it much thought at the time, but at Karen's party, Karen's mom made everyone put their phones in a bowl and they would get them back in the morning. She said she wanted Karen to have an old-fashioned party with no electronic interruption. A lot of the girls whined at first, but they went a long and after the fun began, it was forgotten. But apparently, when it comes to tween girls parting with their social lifelines, rules are made to be broken. The next day at school, there was a little more pointing and whispering than normal from girls. I chalked it up to the slumber party fallout and ignored it. But when boys started pointing, I was suspicious. Why would boys be involved. Missy showed me on her phone that someone took a picture of the bras in the freezer last night and posted it. I guess she was returning my prior kindness.

I didn't realize how many people my age were allowed to engage in social media. During library I asked Miss Appleton if I could use her computer and told her what happened. There it was for all to see with a big arrow pointing to my clearly larger bra and my name Katie Reed. It had been shared through most of the class who have social media. Things stay on the internet FOREVER! If ever I was nearly brought to tears, this was it. I just couldn't believe it, but there it was for all to see. Why would someone do that? And why would they point me out, specifically? I spent the entire hour tracking the post like a Scotland Yard detective. I wanted to know who did this. I found the culprit. It was the twins, Lisa and Laura. They were mad at me because I was chosen for a quartet in the next choir show, instead of them. Was that one song worth this? I was so angry, I started to plot my revenge. I would ask my mom, no demand, I get a social media account. Then I wait and watch them to find something embarrassing and then POUNCE! PICTURE! POST! That would teach them not to mess with me. But then Miss Appleton came up to the desk and placed a printout next to the keyboard of an online article called "Cyberbulling and the Consequences." She didn't say anything at all, just put the papers down and walked away. RBG, it's like she could read my mind, or maybe she saw smoke coming out of my ears. Either way, she's amazing.

I read the article. It talked about cyberbullying causing kids to be killed in revenge for cruel posts or some kids committing suicide from the pain and hurt even years later. Wow. I guess spite is not the way to go. I don't want to be that person or inflict pain. That's not me.I think I'm still going to ask my mom if I can have social media on my phone or just at home on my computer - just to keep an eye out for any posts about me. I'm not being paranoid, but offense is the best defense, as my dad says when he watches football. And awareness is everything. I'm sure you were glad you grew up in the dark age of information. I love computers, don't get be wrong. My mom constantly tells me how lucky we are to be able to research everything and anything at our fingertips right in our own home. She went to the library in her day. You probably did too, RBG. My grandma always says you have to take the good with the bad. Social media adds another layer of good and bad to growing up, whether we want it or not.

Dear RBG:

My grandma always says, "If karma doesn't catch up, God will surely pick up the slack." I admit her sayings often come true. Case in point...(I think that's what you would've said, RBG). A few days ago, there was an unsual and hilarious incident with two seventh graders. I don't know them very well, but I experienced some of their tricks first-hand, as they were among the haters and dodgeball assassins in joint gym. Our school often combined two grades for special intramural tournaments where they randomly selected different grades to be together on teams, to make it fair. Genius idea – that made it fair.

The two seventh graders are "seeing" each other and were kissing in the locker area between classes. Teachers are rarely in that area because it's in between two main hallways, and during passing periods, teachers are posted at specific areas to stand guard and move the flow of traffic along. Someone yelled and kids ran to the sound like moths to the flame. Laughter erupted and then continued in waves as each kid came closer to view. They were kissing, and their braces stuck together. They couldn't move! It was a sight to see. They tried to get apart, but it was no use. They were really stuck.

This was a really big deal. Someone called a teacher, and he tried to get them apart, but nothing worked. A few teachers and the principal gathered to figure out what to do. The principal called the fire department, and the teachers shooed everyone to classes. By the time we got out of class and into the passing hall again, the fire department was still working on them. It took an hour with them locked together until the fire department got them untangled. Word spread quickly, and the entire student body gathered to gawk and laugh at them. You should have seen them. They had to stand there, locked together face to face while everyone laughed. I saw them afterward. The girl's face was wet from crying, and both their faces were still red from panic and humiliation. They had to wait in the principal's office for their parents to come to school. I bet they're both going to need to go back to the dentist to have their braces fixed.

I didn't laugh, but I did smile. I couldn't help myself. It was so funny. I did feel bad for them, it must have been very scary. But after their merciless bullying and teasing, it was a little nice to see them get a taste of their own medicine. That shoe my grandma talked about was on the other foot for sure. It felt a little like justice. You must've felt like that when you won a case, RBG.

Dear RBG:

I thought when I got rid of gym class, that would be the end of my "sports-to-boob ratio" phobia. I was wrong.

Tennis is a problem. I've played tennis since I was in third grade. My mom plays, and we all play on vacations and at the local park district. We even take lessons and play on an intramural team. I'm OK at tennis, and I like it. But now, my boobs get in the way of my double-handed backhand. I have to cross my arms in front of my chest, which is now difficult and sometimes painful. It's definitely affected my swing. If I can get my hand on the racquet, and that's IF, my swing is delayed. My tennis coach says I have to learn a single backhand. I guess I have to. I like the strength of my double backhand. I can really whack it.

Softball has both similar and different problems. My brother and I play on a co-ed softball team. I only play because my dad is the coach, and they needed players. When I bat, my arms cross in front of my chest. I'm learning to hit a little higher, so my arms are away and over my chest. I think that will work, but the other problem happened at the game last weekend.

There's a boy on the team that I kind of like. His name is Greg, and he goes to Catholic school, so we only see each other on the softball field. That has its advantages. He's sweet. He always saves me a spot on the bench next to him. I bat just before him. He almost always hits a home run. He's very good.

At this game, I hit the ball and ran to first and then second base. I'm not the best hitter, but I don't strike out, and I always get on base because I can run fast. I stopped at second base, and Greg batted next. He hit the ball in the outfield, but the game was tight, so I ran as fast as possible to get to home plate. My hat even fell off somewhere around third base. I didn't care. I just ran. When I reached home plate, Greg was right behind me. He smiled and gave me my hat. I didn't know what to do, so I smiled and thanked him. RBG, I couldn't believe he took the time to pick it up around third base and bring it to me. It was gallant

($10 word). Feminism can take a back seat when you're a young girl who wants to get noticed by a boy. Right? Well, I like that attention anyway.

But soon after we sat down on the bench, I started hearing whispers and murmurs. Finally, it got back to me—and Greg. People were pointing and laughing at my boobs going up and down while I was running and a friend told me a boy even whistled. Really? I don't like that kind of attention. It makes me feel very uneasy. I was embarrassed, and so was Greg. So what do I do? Should I run slower and not do my best to avoid ridicule? If I wrap or tape them down, it really hurts, and my mom says it's not good for me. It's just not fair, RBG!!

Dear RBG:

Things are definitely changing with girls and boys. Girls are starting to notice their developing bodies and the importance of makeup and clothes.

Some are even starting to wear a little eye shadow and sparkly lip gloss. I like the sparkly lip glosses, but I really like the ones that come in flavors, like fruits, ice cream, and soda tastes. I like the bubble gum one the best. But, my mom says no eye shadow or any makeup until eighth grade. It's probably best. The girls who wear eye shadow really cake it on. Sometimes it looks like they can barely open their eyelids.

It's weird. Now some girls get giddy around boys they've known for years. And boys look at girls a little differently, sometimes with googly eyes. It's like a game of gossip tag. Girl one tells her friend, girl two, that she likes a boy one. Girl two tells another boy, boy two, who's friends with boy one. Boy two tells boy one about girl one. Then boy two tells girl two boy one's response. Then girl two goes back to girl one with the message – either boy one likes girl one or not. It's exhausting and confusing. There must be an easier way.

My mom says now that I'm a teenager, it's time for some of the firsts—first dances, first boyfriends, first kisses. I don't know about that. We had a few dances at school this year, but mostly the girls all dance with each other, and the boys just sit awkwardly on the sidelines. Some boys dance, but most don't try. I don't know why, but most boys are just not good at dancing. They don't know how to move and definitely don't know what to do with their arms. Girls just watch dancers on TV and copy them. Why don't boys do that? Isn't dancing like sports? You just have to learn how, right?

In our town, we have a roller rink that's pretty popular for birthday parties and school nighttime outings. It's been around forever. My mom skated there when she was a teen. There's not a lot to do in our town, so our school still has roller skating parties there. Only sixth, seventh, and eighth graders in our school get to go. I went to my first one last night. It was so cool.

I don't skate very well. I've only skated a few times. It's so exciting. There's music and colored lights everywhere. The DJ calls out fun games with the songs. Some songs have movements to them, and some have these made-up games to get everyone involved. I was worried about falling, but I went out on the floor and just stayed by the railing. That way if I fell, I could hold onto something. I just couldn't resist the music and games. It was so fun. Even for a lousy skater like me, you could just go slow and put your hands in the air and do the movements like the others. Some people are such good skaters. I want to skate like them. Practice, practice.

Then the DJ played a slow song and called for a "ladies choice" skate. It's when girls ask boys to skate. I was petrified. Asking a boy to dance is one thing, this was different. Not only do you have to be scared of rejection, but if you are me, you're worried that you will fall and be embarrassed in front of everyone. No thanks. But I guess boys go through that all the time when they ask a girl, so I decided to take a chance too. After the first "ladies choice" skate, I got the courage to ask a boy in my class. I was watching him, and he looked like a good skater, which was a plus. You can't have two klutzes out there. I went up to him and asked him. I was so nervous, I wasn't even sure the words came out of my mouth. He said yes and we went out on the floor to skate. Whew!

His name is Robbie. He is so sweet. I held his hand with a white-knuckled death grip so I wouldn't fall, but we both got through the skate in one piece. Afterward, he smiled and thanked me and then went back to his friends. That was the ritual—boys and girls in opposite corners. But he asked me to skate again for the next two couples' skates. That was awesome. And each time we skated, I got a little better and loosened my grip. I'm sure he was grateful for that, but he never even mentioned it.

When I went to sleep that night, my head was in the clouds. Was this just a skating thing? Would he want to see me at school and walk down the hall together? Maybe kiss by my locker? I'm probably getting ahead of myself. Goodnight, RBG.

Dear RBG:

School was interesting today. I watched the clock all day until the time I would see Robbie. We didn't have any classes together, but I see him in the hall at the end of the sixth period. I didn't know what to do after roller skating last night. Should I go up and talk to him? Should I just smile? After daydreaming about our inevitable encounter all day in classes, I decided to let him make the first move. I would walk by him a little slower and smile at him and see what he did. I know this is chickening out, but I see it as a cautious maneuver. And guess what? He stopped and smiled at me and said, "Hi." It's not a lot, but it's a start. I can build on that. Maybe I will smile and wave to him tomorrow.

Wouldn't it be nice to have a boyfriend to walk down the hall with? The only thing is…you see, RBG, I have sweaty hands. Not just when I'm nervous, but they are sweaty, cold, and clammy all the time. It stinks. I spend my days wiping off my hands on my clothes, so my hands don't stick to my school papers and have pen ink transfer onto my hands. And when I wear new jeans, I end up in the girls' bathroom half a dozen times a day to wash the blue dye off my hands. I never had a boyfriend before, so holding hands with someone was not an issue until now. But if the negative reaction of the kids next to me playing "Red Rover" recess games is any indication, this could be an issue. My brother and I have to hold hands in crowds, so we won't get lost. He always whines and says "yuk" when he has to hold my hand. I just tell him to knock it off. He's my brother, I can do that.

Robbie probably didn't realize my hands were sweaty when we held hands skating because I was holding on so tight to avoid falling. I'm sure the pain in his hand threw him off. I'm not really sure what to do about this. I may be getting ahead of myself again. I need to see what happens from here.

Dear RBG:

RBG, the skating party was nice, but pretty much the same. I know this seems silly the way I'm talking about him, but to be honest, I was let down a little bit. Robbie and I skated all the slow songs together. He asked me, I asked him, and after each time, we both went back to our group of friends. It was nice, but I'm just not sure what or where we are. Are we a couple? Does he want to become a couple in the future? Or maybe we're just skating partners? I mean, I'm not looking for a long-term commitment or even "going together." I just don't know what to think. This is all new to me. I just want to know what I should do and how I should act. I'm flying blind here. I waited to see if there was any difference in our hallway encounters the next day, but it was pretty much more of the same. He does stop to say "Hi" now. Then I say "Hi," and we keep going in opposite directions. That's it. Maybe I need to make a move. Or should I just stay on this course? My friend Donna has a boyfriend, I guess—at least that's what she says. They walk to class and lockers together and hang out all night at the skating parties. I asked for her advice, and she told me to have someone we both know talk to him and find out if he likes me. I think that's what spies do in those black-and-white war movies. It seems so silly to resort to spy tactics to find out if a boy is interested. Plus, I'm not sure I'm ready for that. It's so final. I guess this is fine for now. At least I have someone to skate with every week. I know its OK for women to be assertive and make the first move. But is it OK when you're in the sixth grade? What would you have done, RBG? I find myself saying that a lot since I've been writing to you. WWRBGD—what would RBG do? No, I just can't. I think it's best to leave things as they are.

Dear RBG:

A few skating parties have gone by now—no change. I guess I'm not the leave things alone kind of person. This is like torture! I need to know. So, I decided to take Donna's advice. I have a friend in class who has Robbie in a couple of her classes, and I asked her to talk to him. She did…and…he likes me! I'm really excited, and I thought that news would make me feel better, but it doesn't. OK, he likes me. I still don't know what to do. Does this mean we leave notes in each other's lockers? Walk to class? And what do I do now? Should I start it? I don't know if I can. I'm terrified. What if he doesn't want to, even though he likes me? If I start it, and I'm wrong, I <u>will</u> be humiliated. Then I'll have to become a nun. No, really, that's the only option. There's no coming back from that kind of embarrassment. Just add it to the list - one more thing to make me a freak. I hate this!

Update: Today there was a note from Robbie in my locker! It was short but sweet. It said, "Walk to class after lunch? If so, meet me at your locker." What a relief. He made the first move. I know I'm supposed to be strong and liberated like you were, RBG, but when you were in the sixth grade, maybe you were scared and unsure of yourself too?

After lunch, we walked to my next class together. It was nice. I think we were both nervous. We just smiled and looked at each other. We didn't talk, and we didn't hold hands, but it was good. Unfortunately, my class is close to my locker, so it was a short walk. But this is definitely a start—of what, I have no idea, but it's something.

Dear RBG:

Sometimes embarrassment comes from something someone around you does, this time it was my cooky grandparents. While my grandma with the sayings constantly gives me advice, my other grandma always does wacky things.

My brother and Robbie play in the same pony baseball league together, and this week their teams played each other. I had to go to my brother's games, but I usually tried to pop in and watch Robbie's games when I could. All the teams played in the same area on fields that were right next to each other. But this week I didn't have to move. The teams were out on the field warming up, and none of the games had begun. My mom and dad and I were sitting on the bleachers at the furthest ball field when I heard a lot of yelling and a horn beeping. I looked up, and my grandma, Betty, was driving her giant Cadillac over all the ball fields, beeping at the kids to move out of her way. Everyone was yelling at her.

I covered my eyes and looked down. I wanted to shrink into the bleachers and disappear. I could picture myself as liquid melting underneath the bleachers so no one would see me. Another time that invisibility cloak could come in handy. It was like a slow-motion movie or something. She drove over one pitcher's mound then another with her car bumping up and down on each mound. I swear it seemed like time stood still. When she came closer to our field, she was beeping and waiving, calling for my dad, so everyone knew whose grandma she was. Both teams and all the spectators were looking at us and at her and then us again. No one could believe anyone would actually do this. Robbie and the kids on both teams were laughing as she parked her car on the field and flipped open the trunk. She told all the kids to gather around because she had cold drinks and snacks for them. My dad asked her why she drove over the fields.

"The parking lot was too far away and I have all these snacks and drinks for the teams," she explained. "The cooler is heavy and it would have taken several trips. It made more sense to bring the car and the cooler to you."

I do envy one thing about her; she does as she pleases and doesn't let anybody tell her otherwise. That is something to look up to, but maybe it can be accomplished without embarrassing your family.

I was afraid of what Robbie would think. If I had a crazy grandma, maybe I was cookoo too. I looked above my covered eyes and saw Robbie just laughing with his teammates. He saw me looking at him and came over and brought me a drink and a snack.

"Don't worry, Katie," he laughed. "Everyone has a crazy granny. At least she brought cold drinks."

That made me feel better, but I knew the boys would be talking about this in school on Monday. The worst part was my dad had to drive the car all the way back to the parking lot. I'm sure he was uncomfortable too.

Dear RBG:

Robbie and I have been walking in school together for a month now. We even started holding hands last week. It's fun to have a boyfriend. When we walk down the hall together, kids look and some giggle and smile, but now it's a good thing. The giggles and whispers now say, "Wow, she has a boyfriend." Not ridicule, but envy, which is nice for a change. Most girls don't have boyfriends in the sixth grade. It's a big deal! Robbie's a very sweet guy. We leave silly little notes in each other's lockers and text funny videos and emojis to each other after school. We text at night and complain about homework, parents, and brothers. It's nice. I mean, we're not in love or anything, but definitely in "like" with each other. Absolute like.

And last night at the final skating party of the year, he sat with me after couple's skate, and we even skated together during open skate. My skating is getting a little better. I feel more confident and less like I'm one minute from falling every other minute. Robbie's a good skater, and he taught me a few tricks. And guess what, RBG? At the end of the night, he kissed me on the cheek! It was weird. Cool, but weird. He was really nervous, and it was super quick, like a woodpecker pecking at a tree, but he only pecked at me once, of course. It was a surprise. We were just standing there waiting for parent pick up, and he did it. I didn't know what to do? I just smiled at him. I couldn't think of anything to say. But I'm sooo glad my mom didn't see. I really didn't want to answer those questions and make a big deal out of it. My mom would have definitely made a big deal of it.

Ugh! I can't believe it took me all year to get a boyfriend, and now the school year is almost over. I go away to my aunt's for almost the whole summer, so I won't see him much. Well, we can still text, post on social media, and we can Facetime too. We'll figure it out. I think he really likes me. I really like him too. I'm secretly drawing hearts in my notebook R + K 4ever. Who knows? A girl can dream, right?

Suzanne Rudd

7th Grade

"D" Cup: Another Year – Another Size?

Suzanne Rudd

Dear RBG:

Sorry I didn't write over the summer, but my aunt and the twins kept me very busy. The boys are three now, and they get into everything. Even with the two of us, it's hard to keep up. I don't know how she does it during the school year without me. Every time I turn around, they're getting into some mess. When I go to clean it up, they pull things out of cabinets or closets and make another mess. I think they're criminal masterminds in the making. They time everything just right to cause the most mess and chaos. My aunt even put new kid-proof locks on everything to keep them out. The locks didn't even slow them down. Maybe the boys will become safecrackers or something. They're weapons of mass destruction.

They just got out of diapers, and now I have to take them to the potty. No more diaper changes is a relief, but they're boys, so they like to squirt each other and laugh. It's a game, they squirt each other and then try to hit things. My aunt put little targets in the toilet to make it fun for them to go potty, but now they see everything as a bullseye—the walls, the floor, the tub, and me! It's really gross. Now I know why boys in my school do stupid things. They started as babies. I spent most of the summer running after them. Even at the beach, I have to watch them every minute because they run in different directions to confuse us and keep us running after them. I know they do it on purpose, just to torture us. My aunt said no, but I think they know exactly what they're doing. They have double-teaming down to a science. I can't imagine what they will do once they learn more. Scary.

Robbie and I texted and met up on Facetime a few times, but I was glad to see him when I got home.

Luckily he knows some of my friends in his

neighborhood, so I rode my bike over, and we all

hung out. Tina showed us this old kissing game her

mom told her about called "spin the bottle." You

probably knew it, RBG, it's been around forever. We

googled how to play. You sit in a circle and spin a

bottle in the middle. We tried a plastic water bottle,

but that didn't spin well, so Tina went into the

recycling cans in her garage and got an empty wine

bottle. Her parents drink wine a lot. I smelled the

bottle, it stunk. Anyway, one person spins the bottle

and they have to kiss whoever it lands on, no matter

who it is. It's so old school.

I kept hoping it would land on Robbie for me,

but not for anyone else. Most people just gave a peck

on the head or the cheek. I think Tina likes Robbie's

friend, Josh, because her spin landed on him and she

kissed him right on the mouth. The kiss was quick, but

it was on his actual lips. He didn't expect it, based on the look on his face. It was weird, but she just went for it. The only one who landed on Robbie was his friend Tristan. They just looked at each other, laughed, and fist-bumped. I was relieved.

At the end, I think Tina wanted to get the attention away from her and said she was going to spin for me. It landed on Robbie. I'm pretty sure she cheated to make that happen. Everyone chanted, "kiss, kiss, kiss." It was a lot of pressure. He looked a little scared too, so that helped. I leaned over and just kissed him super quick, but it was on the lips. I don't think it counts as a first kiss. Hopefully, our real first kiss will be special with just the two of us, like in the movies. And the music playing in my mind will be romantic and beautiful, not schoolyard chants. When we're ready, it will happen. I can't believe I will start seventh grade with a boyfriend. It's going to be a good year!

Dear RBG:

The inevitable happened. I went school clothes shopping and believe it or not, I need a bigger size bra...again. I thought maybe they would stop growing. After all, I wore a bra all summer to see if I could stay in the "C" cup. But no, I grew again, and now I was into a "D." My mom took me to a corsetiere shop to get measured for a proper bra. She says it's time to have experts measure me to get the right fit.

It's a strange place, the corsetiere shop. They only sell bras and some matching panties, but nothing else. I passed Victoria's Secret in the mall before, but it had fun music and cool different color lights. Everyone's moving around to the music. It was more like a party than a store. The corsetiere shop is much different. It's cold and quiet with very bright lighting—

like a lab or something. It has bras of all kinds and sizes. I saw some really cute ones with different colors, patterns, and shapes. And all kinds of colors, plus zebra and leopard prints, lace, and even some that had bling with fake diamond studs. Some bras are so small, I wonder why someone would bother to wear them. I wouldn't, if I didn't have to. And some bras are huge. I can't imagine wearing a bra that big. They have ones with and without pads. And some have removable flaps. My mom says those are for nursing moms. But, I saw my aunt nursing the twins, and she would just take her bra off completely. Maybe that was because there were two of them, but she didn't nurse them at the same time, so I'm not sure.

We made an appointment online for a fitting. The lady called our name and ushered my mom and I into a large dressing room. The lady, my mom, and I all stood in front of this big mirror while she wrapped a tape measure over me a few times and shouted out numbers to another lady, who pulled bras for me to try on. It was really cramped in that dressing room and felt awkward and a little intrusive ($10 word). It was so impersonal, I felt like a mannequin instead of a real girl. But the lady said it's almost a science when you get into these sizes. The fit of the straps, cup size, wire or no wire, and the hooks in the back or the front are all options, but the styles and colors are limited.

"When you are in this size, fit and support are more important than fancy styles and colors," the corset lady said.

I wish she would stop saying "this size" like it was the most unusual thing in the world. I already feel like a freak. But she explained that if the strap in the back was too tight, I could have back problems. And if the straps were too tight on the top or if I didn't wear underwires, the bones in my shoulder/collar bone could get soft in a spot from the weight, and I could get permanent indentations. Then she showed me the indentations on her shoulder. They looked like a slot big enough to drive a Matchbox car through. So, I chose the uncomfortable wired bra. The wires run under the cup and into the strap on each side, just the right spot to poke under my arm.

The bra is pretty, though. It's white with a flower design and a little bow in the middle. No bling, but at least it has a bow and some lace with a lining, so it doesn't itch. It feels like a straightjacket. And the seams run straight across the middle of the cups. You can see them through my shirt. Now I know why a bra is called an "over-the-shoulder-boulder-holder." With the wires, there is no sag, and everything is high and tight.

I looked it up, a man invented the brassiere. I wonder if it was really invented as a torture device. I could see it. At least the lady made mine a minimizer bra. She said "at this size" you can look smaller. That's the only time I liked it when she said, "at this size." At least something good came out of this. Maybe I will look smaller.

Dear RBG:

Seventh grade is starting off pretty good. I have some new bras, which should make me look like some of the other girls. They're supposed to make you look one cup size smaller. That's still bigger than most girls, but at least it's the same as I was in sixth grade—that's something. My grandma always says you have to take the good with the bad.

Robbie and I walk to class together and leave notes in each other's lockers every day. And we're still texting every night. It's nice. I see more couples this year than before. I think I experience some things ahead of other girls. My grandma says I'm "maturing" faster. Maybe that's why all this happened, my body and mind are just a little more advanced than the others, and everyone else is catching up to me. I'm like a giraffe, standing above the rest of the animals in the jungle, which has advantages, but also makes you stick out. I don't necessarily mind standing out for something I do better than others—I just don't want to stick out for something that's not my fault. I hope this is a sign that I'm blending in, finally.

Dear RBG:

Do I unintentionally self-inflict my own pain? Sometimes I wonder if I'm my own worst enemy. This week I began to wonder. We're studying smoking and what it does to the lungs in Health class. Our teacher, Mr. Collins, showed us a picture of some lungs that were damaged due to a lifetime of smoking. It looked like the lung X-rays I had last year when I had walking pneumonia. Being an overachieving B+ student, I brought my x-rays into Health class for some brownie points and a little extra credit. OK, it was a "brown-noser" move, but pretty harmless—right? I bet you did a lot of special projects and extra credit in class, RBG, that's how you got so smart. The teacher showed them against the window of the classroom to show the gunk in my lungs. He tried to explain how smoking damaged the lungs way more than my pneumonia showing the different areas of the lung x-ray, but it was hard to hear the teacher with all the kids yelling "gross" and "yuk." So childish. I felt pretty proud of my classroom contribution until the teacher showed the side x-ray. My teacher, Mr. Collins, is very into science, more than anyone in the classroom, times 100. He's always so excited to show us how things work and how everything in the universe fits together, but I don't think a lot of the kids care. I feel bad for him, but health and science are not big interests of mine, or my best subjects. That's why I need the extra credit points.

Mr. Collins was too into his lesson to notice, and I was sitting like a proud peacock listening intently, when I began to hear the "yuk" and "gross" yells end and whispers and snickering begin. Slowly like the wave at a ballgame, one person at a time started to snicker, point, and look at the next person, and so on and so on. I couldn't figure out what was so funny. Puzzled, finally I looked up at the window and my side view x-ray. Yes—you could see the shape of my titanic breasts in the negative view of the x-ray. How could I be so stupid? I just handed them the fuel to ignite a ridicule fire. The seconds seemed like hours as I was chanting to myself to try and make a psychic connection with the teacher "put it down, put it down." Luckily, he mercifully finished the lesson, but by lunch, the rest of the school knew. The cafeteria was a hushed chorus of laughter and pointing, but to me it sounded like an enormous choir harmonizing "sideboob" at the top of their lungs. One of the more creative boys in the class coined that name, which I heard many times that day. After lunch, when I was walking down the hall with Robbie, I could barely hold it together. The whispers, giggles, and points continued in the hallway. I didn't want him to know. It was bad enough for those hyenas, but if he did it too, I couldn't take it. I was nearly in tears, so I told him I had to go to the bathroom and would see him after school by the busses. We usually met there after school. Then I went into the bathroom and waited until most of the kids were in class. I left just in time to make it to my next class. My pride wasn't worth a tardy, but I figured less people, less problem. I endured that one mistake and the new nickname for almost a week. That definitely wasn't worth the extra credit points.

Dear RBG:

Things are looking up. Luckily, Robbie was oblivious ($20 word) to my embarrassment, or at least he didn't mention it. Besides, there are more exciting things to look forward to. This week, the school put up posters for the Halloween Costume Dance. My first real dance!!! And I have a date! Plus, we can wear costumes. This cannot get better. Happily, the school is buzzing with plans for the dance, and my x-ray catastrophe is yesterday's news. As my grandma says, "Thank goodness for small miracles."

The dance is really exciting like a real date. Skating parties were nice, but this is dancing—my turf now. I've been taking dancing lessons since I was five years old. I'm proficient ($15 word) at jazz and choreography, and I can tap. I struggle through ballet, but I know the positions. Ballet requires more balance than I can usually muster, especially now. My top-heavy body isn't exactly built for ballet. I have a hard time keeping on my toes without falling over. I'm not exactly sure if that's why my balance is off, but my dance teacher told me that most ballerinas are not built like me. No crying over spilt milk here, as my grandma says. Now I'm advanced, so I can just take tap and jazz, no more ballet. Plus, I love dancing to pop music. Dancing is the best part of slumber parties.

Since some people have dates and some don't, it probably won't be a couple's thing. But I do have a date, so I thought it would be cute to do a couple's costume. I asked Robbie about costumes, and he wanted to wear the stormtrooper costume he already had. He's a huge Star Wars fan, so I wore a Princess Leia costume. The costume was bulky, and the hair was uncomfortable. You've seen it, RBG, it's like two earmuffs. Whoever thought this was a good idea? Personally, I'm not a *Star Wars* fan, but I saw every movie with my brother, so I'm familiar. It isn't the kind of couple I was looking for, but I thought it would be nice to be supportive. At least people will know we're together. I'm so excited for this dance, I can't wait!!

Dear RBG:

The dance was sooooooo cool! I really didn't know what to expect. I knew what the gym would look like because I helped decorate it after school for the last two weeks. I think we did a good job. It was a typical spooky Halloween theme, so there were tombstones, skulls, and cobwebs, etc., everywhere. It looked nice, but when the dancing colored lights and fog machine were added, it really came to life.

The DJ played some of the typical Halloween tracks like *Monster Mash, Thriller,* and *I Put A Spell on You* from my favorite vintage Halloween movie, *Hocus Pocus.* I'm surprised how old some of that music is but still fun. And they played some more recent hits, too. The dancing was not what I expected. I was ready for the kind of raucous and out-of-control jumping around at slumber parties or even the structured but joyous moves of our after-performance dance studio parties. This was different. It was mostly girls. Most boys and some girls stayed on the sidelines huddled in the corner or spent most of the time in the adjacent cafeteria where the food was. Some boys danced, but a lot of them seemed really uncomfortable. I guess it's like the girl and boy camp divisions at skating parties, but at least the guys skated all the time. Maybe boys don't know how to dance.

Robbie was so sweet, he tried to dance with me and some of the girls, but I could tell it was not his thing. He had this awkward blank stare while he shuffled his feet back and forth. It was painful to watch. So I let him off the hook and told him to get some food, and I would come in after a few more dances. A half an hour later, I got thirsty and decided to go to the cafeteria. I didn't mean to take so long, but I was having too much fun to leave the dance floor. Soon, more people were eating than dancing in the gym, so the teachers and chaperones told everyone to go back into the gym. They played some slower songs and said it was ladies choice, just like at the roller rink. I think boys only dance if girls ask them. Slow dancing was easy for them, since it was a uniform-type dance. The guy puts both his arms around the girl's waist and the girl puts her hands around the guy's neck.

The teachers were all watching to ensure some space was between each pair. One of the teachers walked around telling people she wanted to see light between them. This is seventh grade, so it's not really an issue. It was then I became all too aware of my added appendages. My boobs did get to his chest pretty fast. He's tall, that's a good thing. Otherwise my boobs would have been above his chest. Yikes, that would've been worse. At first, he kept some distance; I think he was aware of them too. Eventually, we started to relax and get closer. And then, he leaned toward me and kissed me! A real kiss! It was spectacular. I think I heard fireworks and trumpets sound, but I'm sure it wasn't in my head. It was the perfect moment.

Dear RBG:

One of the great things about Jr. High is all the clubs and activities. I like choir, band, yearbook, and school newspaper, but the one that really knocks me out is theatre. I've been in choir and dance for years, and I love musicals. I tried out for a musical which satires *Aesop's Fables*. It's cute; all the actors dress up like animals in different fables. I got the role of one of the sheep sisters. I'm so excited. We get to sing, dance, and act. I always secretly wanted to be an actress someday or a judge, like you, RBG, or maybe president. I still can't decide. But I'm thrilled to be in the play and test out my acting skills.

The only bummer was the costume fittings the other day. It was a combination of the nightmares from the corsetiere bra fittings and a mirror of the slumber party frozen bra drama. Our school tried to stretch the drama department budget (never the sports budget, though) by keeping costumes from former productions that could be resized, recycled, and reused in different time periods and places. So the volunteer costume moms called all the girls into a room to measure us. One mom measured and called out the measurements to another mom, who wrote them down. As I heard each girl's measurements, I felt like a lamb to the slaughter. I know my measurements from the bra fittings, so I could compare. It was horrifying and humiliating. I just waited in line, knowing that my size would be much larger than all the other girls. Each size called was a clear reflection and all too glaring reminder of the differences between the other girls and me. The closer I got to the front of the line, I started to sweat and I was having difficulty breathing. I really thought I would pass out. And sure enough, when she took my measurements, 42" chest, the other mom said, "Did you say 42 inches? I don't know if we have anything that big?" Really? Not only did she say it out loud and then repeat it, but then she made a comment about how big it is. I know she didn't mean it, but it's completely insensitive. Once again, I feel like a circus freak. But then it got worse. The first mom said, "We might have something that big. Remember that big fat girl we had a few years ago? Maybe one of her costumes will work if we take in the bottom and leave the top big."

I couldn't believe they were having this conversation right in front of me and in the middle of a room with a bunch of other girls. I know they weren't trying to be mean, but did they have any idea how degrading they were being, not only to me but to this other girl or any other girl with body-image issues? They were talking as if it was what color hair we had, a matter of fact. But tall, short, fat, skinny, or big are subjective opinions, not facts. And body-shaming is never OK. I know they probably didn't realize what they were doing, but after all, these were moms!

Moms are supposed to know how to act. My face must have been so red that everyone could see my embarrassment, but I held back the tears. I escaped further debasing ($5 word) when one of the moms told me to go into the costume room, look around, and try on a few things to see if they fit. I didn't hear any giggles or snickers, so I don't know if the other girls said anything as my back was turned to them. I was so in my head, the only thing I could hear was the moms and my fast-beating heart.

Alone in the costume room, I was able to calm myself a little. I almost thought of quitting the play, but no. I'm not going to let some thoughtless people rob me of the opportunity to do something I really wanted to do. I would persevere ($10 word). Turns out this "big fat girl" was in a lot of plays and had really nice costumes. One of the moms took pity on me and came into the room to help me find some good costumes.

She smiled and said, "When we take in the bottom of the dress, you will have a nice little figure here." I didn't exactly know what she meant by that, but at least I got a nice costume of it. Just like Blanche Dubois, "I always rely on the kindness of strangers." I saw that in an old black and white movie on TV.

Dear RBG:

Since the dance, Robbie and I are in a routine. The first kiss is a step in a new direction, but after all, this is pretty much it for a couple in seventh grade. It's all I want anyway. I have a boyfriend who gives me a kiss once and a while, so that's enough for me. Actually, all the boys in our grade seem to be maturing, a little. More guys and girls walk down the hallway together and hold hands. There's less bullying and dopey making fun of girls. And they show more interest in girls and actually talk to them like normal people. All steps in the right direction. But I find that all boys are not at the same level.

Some weird boy from my Health class is making strange gestures and noises when he sees me. Yesterday he called me Arthur and laughed. His name is Elliot. He did the same thing today, so I asked one of the Robbie's friends from the same class to find out what his deal is. You'll never believe it, RBG. I still can't believe it. Robbie's friend gave me a drawing he did of a girl with big boobs, I guess it was supposed to be me, with her hands cupped in front of her boobs. Underneath it said, "Arthurites."

What a jerk! And stupid too, as he misspelled arthritis and only had three fingers on each hand. How low can you go? And what's even worse, I saw Robbie's friend snicker a little when he got the drawing. Will some things never change? I decided to take the high road and ignore the idiot caveman. But after school, Robbie was different. Quieter than usual, and he seemed sad. I asked him what was wrong, and he said his buddies told him about Elliot. They all have gym and practice for park district indoor soccer together. I could see he was angry but also a little embarrassed. He didn't have as much experience as I did with ridicule and bullying. I'm very familiar with it and still can't handle it completely. Robbie is shy and didn't really want to get into it with another boy or be singled out by his team. He said he wanted to defend me and was going to pound Elliot after soccer practice. At first, I swooned a little. He wants to defend me—like a fairy-tale prince come to my rescue. I quickly awoke from that cartoon fantasy and told him I already had a plan to handle it. The truth is—I had no idea what to do.

All night I devised several different plans. After all, I'm not a damsel in distress. I need to be able to handle this situation myself. I've put up with this nonsense for years, but I think it's about time I fight back. I'm not going to let some tiny-brained moron mess up my perfect boyfriend situation.

Today after school, I was at the park district for tennis practice. The soccer field Robbie and the other boys play on is next to the tennis courts. They put nets in between the two areas when play starts. At first I decided to go up to Elliot and use superior words to shame and embarrass him into submission. But I chickened out. So I decided to go with Plan B. I saw Elliot with a few other guys on the soccer field before practice, so I went out on the tennis court early with a bucket of balls. The nets were not up yet, so I decided to bean Elliot with a bunch of tennis balls. I've been playing tennis for years, and I can usually put the ball exactly where I want. I was really mad. I sent

a couple of balls "accidentally" into the soccer field,

and then I pummeled him with a few balls, one right

after another. He kept yelling over to me, but I was

possessed. With each ball I hit, I could see his dumb

face and crude drawing and just let it go. After hitting

him with five balls, he called me Arthur and came over

to me with his hands cupped in front of his chest, like

his drawing. That was it. It was like an out-of-body

experience. Years of pent up anger at all the bullying,

giggles, snickering, whispers, and name-calling gave

me a mission. You would've been proud of me, RBG.

I spun a web of well-crafted insults and threw in a lot

of $20 and $25 words from my book. He didn't even

know what hit him.

"Very funny—ha ha. How long did it take for

you to come up with that brilliant and erudite

nickname? A day? No, I bet it took weeks. I hope you

don't have a test tomorrow as this may have used up all your brain cells. Oh, that's right, with that tiny brain, you probably have smoke coming out of your ears all the time from overuse. I hope it's not a health class because you will fail anatomy. From your drawing, you obviously don't know how many fingers go on a human hand. But I'm sure you're used to failing. After all, you can't even spell arthritis. It's one of those big, tough multi-syllabic words for which your pea brain has no aptitude. Maybe you should play less sports as the excess testosterone from either soccer or your natural prepubescence is cutting off what little intelligence you can muster in that Neanderthal mind. But not to worry, you can get a job. You certainly won't matriculate at any institute of higher learning. Can you say, 'Would you like a large fries and drink with your order?' All those words are monosyllabic, so you should be just fine."

RBG, it was like in a movie. I said it in one continuous breath and didn't stop. He was dumbfounded. I turned and went back to my tennis court without looking back. It was great. The boys were laughing at him, and the girls were clapping for me. Vindication!! I didn't even remember everything I said. It was like a blur, but someone watching posted a video on social media. "Tennis Girl Pummels Soccer Guy." One million views and likes! I didn't see Robbie come out of the locker room until I was back on my court. He stood there until I saw him and smiled at me. I know it will be fine now. I can take care of myself.

Dear RBG:

Well, Robbie and I broke up. It's been strange for a while now, so it was pretty mutual. I'm not devastated or anything. I think we were kind of bored with each other. We'll still be friends, I think. I don't know, maybe the tennis/soccer incident was too much for him. He never mentioned it after that day, but the guys may have been teasing him. I guess he doesn't have tough skin like I do. Maybe I'm just used to it. It could be something else, too. I mean, it's only seventh grade, it's not like we were going to get married. Plus, I'm so involved in my new activities, I really don't mind. He was my first boyfriend, after all. My mom said the "bloom was off the rose." I have no idea what that one means, but I'm looking forward to my next boyfriend, soon.

At the last dance of the year, some of my new theatre friends and I made up some line dances to popular songs. People really liked them. We got noticed, and a boy named Kenny came up to me and asked me to slow dance. Then another boy named Greg asked me to slow dance too. I had a lot of fun.

Maybe I don't need only one boyfriend after all. Can you have more than one at a time?

The play was great. I think I was pretty good. The costumes, the lights, the applause from the audience, and the rush of performing were all very cool. I never experienced such elation before. I can't wait to do it again. And I met so many new friends. Theatre kids just seem more accepting and less judgmental. The kids in that group are all different, but everyone seems to ignore that. It just doesn't matter. We all like performing, and we're all kids. We have that in common. That's nice.

Suzanne Rudd

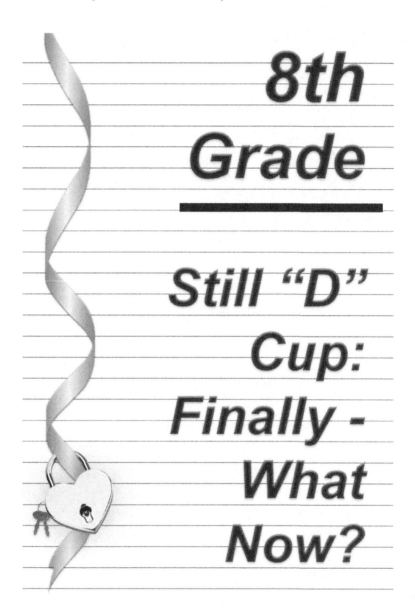

8th Grade

Still "D" Cup: Finally - What Now?

Dear RBG:

I spent a lot of the summer at the beach with the twins, my Aunt, and Suz. I'm turning fourteen this summer, and both Suz and I had a different attitude toward the boys on the beach this year. We spent most of the time laying on blankets and walking on the beach watching boys and just trying to get noticed. Last summer wasn't the right time, but this summer, I already had a boyfriend under my belt, so I was ready for a little attention. I watched some of the older girls flirt with boys and studied what they did, with mental notes like I would be tested on it.

Flirting is an interesting game. Girls try to get attention with their tans and bikinis while doing practically nothing, just laying around or walking up and down the beach. Boys try to get attention by swimming, body-surfing, and playing football, Frisbee, and volleyball. And somehow the ball or Frisbee always ends up on the blanket of a girl. Then they apologize and talk to the girl. That is so obvious but effective. The conversations are really about nothing—school, music, movies, and TV are all possible talking points. But all are discussed with the boy laughing and smiling and the girl laughing, smiling, and tossing her hair around.

It was strange, but Suz and I tried to apply what we learned. Let's just say, we weren't good at it, RBG. We said one awkward thing after another– and there was way too much laughing and hair tossing. We sounded like hyenas. But, either way, it was fun. I guess it takes time and practice to be good at flirting. I can't wait to use more of it in eighth grade. There are more dances, rolling skating parties, and maybe some boy-girl birthday parties. I'm looking forward to that. I think the more boys get interested in girls, like a girlfriend, the teasing will stop. Everyone is maturing. That is a very good thing.

Dear RBG:

On the last weekend at my aunt's house, I got a big surprise. This year is my golden birthday, the fourteenth of August, and I turned fourteen. My mom, grandma, and aunt set up a fun girl's weekend to celebrate. And my uncle took the twins fishing with my dad and brother. That was interesting. I don't know if they can handle two kids on a boat or anywhere else by themselves. Luckily, the twins only came back dirty.

The girl's weekend was a blast. One day we went to a spa and got facials, manicures, and pedicures. The ladies there did way better than the job I do on my nails. I can never seem to get the nail polish on the nail without getting some on the sides. They must use some super polish or something because my nails shine and sparkle now. I almost don't want to get my hands wet again, so they stay that way forever. But I can't. I want to swim at the beach, and I have to shower and wash my hair every day, plus helping with dishes and the babies. I will just enjoy them while they last.

We went to the beach all day and played cards way into the night. Cards are a big deal in my family. We even have several family card games that everyone plays. I don't know if they're real card games or just made up, but I was happy when I was old enough to learn them and invited to play with the grownups. I'm good at cards. I'm really fast and, since I'm younger and wear glasses, I can see the cards from the middle of the table. That helps. Playing cards also gives you time to talk, really talk. I told them some of my stories from school, and they told me their stories. It was a real education. They always try to impart wisdom on me, whether I liked it or not. But this time, it made me feel a little better like I was one of the girls.

I don't know why I never noticed, but "big boobs" run in my family. My mom, aunt, and grandma experienced some similar episodes when they were growing up. It was nice to feel I wasn't alone, and there may be better things to come. Although, none of them started in the fourth grade like I did. They also told me a little about what to expect in the future.

My mom said she blossomed later in high school. She had the same problem finding clothes to fit. For a two-piece bathing suit or work suit, she needed to find different sizes for the top and bottoms, which was always a challenge. She even had to buy her wedding dress a couple of sizes larger and have it tailored down at the waist and shoulders to fit.

She said when she was pregnant, her boobs were huge. She wore G and H cup bras. I didn't even know women wore them that big. Did they have bras in all the letters of the alphabet? That's practically in a different time zone. I was terrified mine would do that. That's why she knew to go to the special bra corsetiere store.

Now she thinks of them in more practical terms. The bra is big enough to be a convenient place to carry money, credit cards, and ID without a purse—just tuck it in the bra. And she uses it as a shelf to prop up her Ipad or book to read. Ewww. Too much information!

She laughed and admitted now she's in an F cup size, but the bra companies call it DDD, so women don't feel as bad. An A, B, C, and D are the size stated. But E is often labeled as DD, F is DDD, but larger sizes like G and H are marked G and H? So confusing.

She did warn that it's a bit of a crumb catcher, as she often finds potato chips, cereal, or popcorn in her bra at the end of the night. That happens to me too. Something happens when I put my fingers to my mouth—a lack of eye-hand coordination, I guess.

I never really saw my aunt in the "big boob" club. Maybe they deflated after she had the babies. I mean, she breast-fed both of them for almost two years. They drink regular milk now, but maybe they dried hers up. She's the family rebel and my feminist compass. She loved having big boobs. She said she would flaunt them and use them to get her way with boys. That was a big surprise to me. I love the empowerment of it all, but it seems inauthentic ($25 word).

When she was a sophomore in high school, she wanted to date seniors because they could drive, which made dating a whole lot easier. No mom and dad driving and picking up. That makes sense. She said the "boobs" made her look older and gave her an hour-glass figure. Oh, that's what the costume moms meant. Now, I get it.

Her senior boyfriend, Kurt, was a football player. She called him "pretty, but dumb." She said a box of rocks had more to say than this guy. All he could talk about was football and every conversation somehow magically went right back to football.

She got him to notice her with a trick. She leaned over a little bit when seated next to him so her boobs were right on his arm. Yuck. Gross. Too much sharing!!!

Even though my mom and grandma tried to shush her, they laughed like they understood. I guess big boobs are a thing with older boys. I don't know why. What's so great about them? I sure don't like them. Guess you have to be a guy to understand.

My aunt marches to her own drummer. That's one of the reasons I love spending summers with her. She is so different from anyone I know. She told me that God only gave things to people who could handle them. She said women had to use what they could to shift the balance of power in their favor. And she used them whenever she wanted to get her way. To get ahead in a line. To get served faster at a bar. To get out of a speeding ticket. To get a taxi. But when she told me how she pulled her ID from her cleavage to get past the doorman at a club, my grandma put her cards down and got dead silent. That was it.

I thought my aunt was going to get a lecture on corrupting a young girl. But instead she pulled down the sleeve of her shirt and showed the crevasses in her shoulders from wearing bras and said, "You think this is funny?"

I did not think that was funny. They were huge. Forget matchbox cars, like the corsetiere lady, you could fit real car tires in those dents. I wish I had a mind eraser to wipe my memory of that moment. You can never unsee some things. I would never complain again about the discomfort of the underwires if it kept me from having those.

"Weren't you one of those bra burners in the '70s?" my aunt defended herself. Oh, that is too much to see, sensory overload. I just closed my eyes and kept hoping; please don't let that be true. Say no, say no!

My grandma laughed and said no. Thank goodness! But then she said she was so big then, it would have been criminal to unleash those things on the public without a bra—double eeww. I didn't know if I could take much more.

Everyone laughed, and my grandma said that with her weight and age, she was into the G size. She said if she got that breast reduction surgery, she could probably lose 30 lbs. Yikes! They weigh 30 lbs? Is that possible?

For the first time, I really looked at my Grandma's boobs. They did hang very low. I always thought it was her clothes, but her boobs were at her waist and rested on her legs when she sat down. I definitely did not want that—not ever. I would wear a bra 24/7 if I could avoid that slip and slide.

Gram got really somber. My aunt and mom did too. They didn't know I knew this, but my grandma's sister is a breast cancer survivor, but she didn't keep her breasts. Too close. They didn't want to scare me, but I had overheard my aunt and mom talking about it.

"We all have our crosses to bear," my grandma said. I heard her say that about a million times. I think it was her favorite saying, as she seemed to use it for a number of circumstances. But for the first time, it rang true.

Over the last few years, I would jump at the chance to be more "normal" and not have big boobs. I could have been one of the many girls going through average puberty in my school. But listening to the women in my family, it seemed they all traveled a similar road with different paths but had no regrets.

I guess you are the way you are made, for better or worse, but I could have done without the worse part. That reminds me of a gem in my grandma's bag of sayings—the good with the bad. If you didn't have any bad, you wouldn't know what good was. I still have a long way to go, but maybe the difficult times helped make me feel a little more comfortable in my own skin. I guess it makes me what

I'm now and for the future. I'm not changing for

anyone—most of all myself. It's just me.

****

Growing Up Girls Series – What's Next?

The *Growing Up Girls Series* of books tells the stories of different girls ages 8-16 who struggle to fit in and embrace themselves because of bullying, teasing and expectations put on them by others.

In the next book in the series *The One and Only Skizitz*, Skizitz and Emmy showed us how there are many different kinds of bullies, but you can rise above them by celebrating yourself. #BEYOURSELF.

The third book in the series *Popularity* introduces sixteen year-old Meredith. She watches the popular kids in school with envy and is desperate to join them. She'll do anything to be accepted, so she denies her own truth and puts herself on the shelf to become who they want.

Future books in the series will meet *Chatty Cathy* and *Nerdy Norah*, both try to deal with growing up and the challenge to #BEYOURSELF with those who try to keep them down.

Subscribe to my newsletter or follow me on social media (links on the next page) for news and sneak peeks on these books.

About the Author:

Suzanne Rudd Hamilton

Thank you for reading this book. I hope you liked the heart and the humor, but also the hope.

I spent my first career trying to find my bliss in journalism, public relations, real estate, and marketing. Now I'm enjoying my second career writing fictional mystery and romance novels, youth and children's books, stories, essays, and plays to tell stories of everyday life experiences in a fun-filled read. Born in Chicago, me and my computer, along with my husband and dog, are happy transplants in the warm and gentle breezes of Southwest Florida.

My Other Works...

Welcome to my world. I write in books for middle grades and young adults, but I also write romances and mysteries for adults and children's illustrated books under a couple derivatives of my name. Even my adult books are clean and friendly for any audience. If you want to read more from me, here are my works. All novels are available in paperback and ebook on Amazon.com and Kindle and soon to be available audiobooks through Amazon.com/Audible:

Middle-Grade/Young Adult: Suzanne Rudd

Growing Up Girls Series:

– *Diary of 6th Grade "C" Cup*

– *The One and Only Skizitz*

Children's Picture Books : Suzanne Hamilton

– *How An Angel Get's Its Wings*

Historical Romance: Suzanne Rudd Hamilton

Current Series:

A *Timeless* American Historical Romance

– The Sailor and The Songbird

Cozy/Detective Mystery: Suzanne Rudd Hamilton

Beck's Rules Mysteries Series:

– *Beck's Rules*

Secret Senior Sleuths Society:

– Puzzle at Peacock Perch (release October 2021)

I also write plays for the performing arts: *Hollywood Whodunnit, Death, Debauchery and Dinner, Dames are Dangerous* and *Puzzle at Peacock Perch* and the new musical *Welcome Home.*

Social Media:

Feel free to reach out to me and sign up for my newsletter to get bonus materials, name and book cover contests, giveaways, and exclusive updates on new releases. I love to hear from my readers. You can sign up and find out what I'm working on and read some of my recent short stories and books at www.suzanneruddhamilton.com.

Check out my YouTube channel for my segment "Book Talk: Behind the Pages" with interviews with authors and experts about the rocky road of growing up. Also follow me on social media at:

@suzanneruddhamilton

@suzanneruddhamilton

@suzruddhamilton

Suzanne Rudd Hamilton, Author

@suzanneruddhamilton

@suzanneruddhamilton

Made in United States
North Haven, CT
21 January 2024

47733645R00098